GUILT
by DEFAULT

RJ Barclay

Imprint: Indies United Publishing House, LLC
Paperback ISBN: 978-1-64456-728-9
Kindle ISBN: 978-1-64456-729-6
ePub ISBN: 978-1-64456-730-2

Library of Congress Control Number: 2024908195

Front Cover Design by Tatiana Vila of Vila Design
Formatted by The Book Khaleesi

*I wish to thank every person
who encouraged and supported me
on this journey.*

I am forever grateful.

Chapter 1

2004

John Quisenberry raised his arms overhead and stretched side-to-side. The brisk morning air sent an invigorating chill through his body. Homer, close behind, charged through his legs nearly knocking him off balance. "Whoa, Buddy," he laughed. The bulldog sniffed the yard's perimeter, searching for a place to pee, as John meandered down the driveway to retrieve the morning newspaper. Across the street, the neighbor's garage door rumbled open. *Oh great.*

Craig backed his red convertible out of the driveway and stopped in front of John's house. He stuck his crew-cut head over the side of the car and gave him a condescending look. "Hey, Quisenberry!" he called out. "I see you're enjoying those bankers' hours." John bristled and tightened his bathrobe. Craig liked to boast that his position as Commander in the Coast Guard made him more of a man.

John threw him a mock salute. "Sure am!" He picked up the paper and whistled for the dog. Homer raced him up the driveway. John entered the house breathing in the scent of French Roast. He poured dog chow into Homer's bowl and scratched him behind his ear. "Here you go, Pal," he murmured. "Good boy." Smiling, John grabbed his "World's Greatest Dad" mug from the dish rack. The kids presented him with a huge box last year on his forty-fifth birthday. Once unwrapped, he'd discovered a series of smaller boxes, each nestled inside the other. By the time he got to the mug, wrapping paper covered the floor. The kids had bellowed with laughter as Homer ran through the house trailing ribbons.

John filled his mug and slurped the hot liquid. He savored this morning ritual when all was quiet. Once the kids were awake, it would be chaos until bedtime. Pulling up a chair, he spread the newspaper onto the table and glanced at the headlines. "Sex Offender Registry Goes Public!" His heart stopped. *Oh, no, no, no.* Water pipes banged. His oldest daughter was getting into the shower—the whole family would be up soon. He scanned the article for pertinent information. "People in the state of California now have online access to names and addresses of registered sex offenders." *Fuck.*

"Hi, Daddy!" Lucy, their youngest, burst into the kitchen. John sprang from the chair. His wife, Melissa, would be close behind. He folded the newspaper and stuck it on the counter behind some tool catalogs. Lucy wore pink leggings under an even pinker dress embroidered with balloons. Her strawberry blonde hair stuck straight up in a scrunchy, resembling a cartoon character. She bounded over for a hug. He wrapped his arms around her. "Hey, pink girl." Beads of sweat broke out on his forehead. "Ready for breakfast?"

"Can I have Cheerios with bananas?" Her blue eyes glimmered.

John tugged her ponytail. "You betcha!" He glanced at the newspaper peeking out from behind the stack, praying Melissa wouldn't ask about it.

His wife made her way to the coffeepot, hair tousled from sleep. She wore a baggy T-shirt that said *I Just Need to Go to Jazzercize!* Her mismatched pajama bottoms had seen better days. "Morning, Hon," John said. He forced a smile and kissed her cheek. "Sleep okay?"

"Pretty good." She yawned. "You?"

"I slept great!" His tone was an octave too high—too enthusiastic. Did she notice? *Just paranoid.* He poured Lucy's cereal, and with shaky hands, sliced a banana. He set the bowl in front of her.

"Thanks, Daddy," she said.

The scent of strawberry shampoo wafted into the room. Thirteen-year-old Diana strode into the kitchen wearing a green hoodie with skinny jeans. Her auburn hair, the color of Melissa's, fell halfway down her back. John bit his lip when he noticed her darkened lashes. Since the start of middle school, Diana changed from a free-spirited tomboy to a moody teen. She opened the refrigerator, took out a carton of peach yogurt, and peeled back the wrapper. He watched as she licked the foil and tossed it into the trash. His stomach clenched. *What if my name is on that list?* She grabbed her backpack. "I have practice after school today."

"Will you be home in time for dinner?" Melissa asked. "I'm making spaghetti."

"Yes, Mom, I'll be home by six." John glimpsed the eye roll behind his wife's back. "Marie's here. Bye!"

Melissa cringed when the door slammed. She looked at John, eyes narrowed. "Are you okay? You seem a little off."

He couldn't get into it now. Not with Kevin coming through any minute. "Thinking about work stuff, I guess."

Like clockwork, their fifteen-year-old son entered the kitchen. "Did you get more bagels?"

"I did," Melissa said.

Kevin clomped across the floor, banging the cupboard shut after he retrieved the package. He split a bagel in half and popped the pieces into the toaster. Opening the refrigerator wide, he tossed a box of cream cheese on the counter and grabbed the carton of orange juice. He removed the lid, took a long gulp, and wiped his mouth with the back of his hand.

Melissa glared at him; lips pursed.

Kevin ignored her. He grabbed the bagel from the toaster and loaded it up. John joked with him, "Hey Kev, would you like some bagel with your cream cheese?"

"Ha-ha, funny, Dad."

Their son resembled John more each day. Unlike his sisters, Kevin inherited John's dark hair and brown eyes. He already stood eye-to-eye with him. *What if he finds out about me?*

Kevin slung his backpack over his shoulder and grabbed his skateboard. Bagel in hand, he headed to the door. "I'm going to the skate park with Cole after school today." He glanced at Melissa. "Yes, Mom, there will be plenty of time for homework when I get home."

"Dinner at six," she called after him.

The door slammed.

Mel glanced at John, shaking her head. They turned to Lucy, so quiet, her presence went undetected at times. She attended the afternoon kindergarten class, allowing John to spend time with her while Melissa showered. Today though, he patted her head, swallowing the lump in his throat. "Lucy Goose, Homer looks ready to go outside. Can you please take him to the backyard?"

Melissa turned to him and raised her brow.

Lucy hopped from her chair. "Come on, big boy." The dog trotted beside her.

"Grab your jacket," Melissa said. "It's chilly." She turned back to John, her eyes a question.

"The registry is online," he croaked.

"What?" Mel's face drained of color. "How do you know?" Her voice, breathy and shrill, sounded on the verge of hysteria.

John gestured to the newspaper behind the catalogs. "Front page."

Melissa stood and hurried from the kitchen. John knew she'd gone to get her computer. He put his head in his hands. The rape and murder of seven-year-old Megan Kanka in 1994 attracted national attention. The perpetrator, a registered sex offender, lived nearby. One month later, New Jersey's General Assembly passed the bill known as Megan's Law. The law intended to inform members of the public about the presence of sex offenders in the community.

John and Melissa lived in Vallejo at the time — Kevin and Diana were just toddlers. He took a plea bargain eleven years prior, with the understanding his name would remain confidential. The new law threatened to expose John's past conviction. Only perpetrators deemed "high risk" were revealed, but for months, they lived in fear of exposure. It had been the toughest time of their marriage. *Until now.*

Years passed, and John thought the worst was behind them. Then, in 2003, the PROTECT Act (Prosecutorial Remedies and Other Tools to End the Exploitation of Children Today) was signed by George W. Bush. This required all states to maintain a database of registered sex offenders for use in background checks. Soon after, the demand came for the public to access the list. Last month, September 2004, Governor Schwarzenegger signed AB 488 into law, making the database public via a website known as Megan's Law.

Melissa returned with the laptop. Her leg jiggled as the computer hummed to life. "What do I look up? Does it list a website? Do I type in *Megan's Law*?" The clicking of the keyboard got faster, louder, echoing through the kitchen. "Damn it!" she swore. "I keep getting an error message!"

"What does it say?" John asked.

"HTTP 429. Too many people accessing the site."

"That couldn't be right," John said. "Maybe it's just a glitch." He hoped to God she wasn't right.

The sharp ring of the phone pierced the room. Melissa leaped to answer it. "Donna?" She recognized her sister's number on the Caller ID.

John heard undecipherable squawking.

"I've been trying to log on," Mel groaned, "but haven't been able to get through." Her hand trembled as she clung to the receiver. "Oh, God! What does it say?"

A darkness descended upon him—the walls closing in.

Melissa hung up and sank to the floor. Her shoulders wracked with sobs.

He pulled his chair next to her and laid a hand on her back, barely touching her, as if she might break. "Honey," he whispered.

"it'll be okay." *So fucking inadequate.* The heaviness of her despair radiated through his body as if it were his own. John prided himself on being the man of the family, the protector. How could he protect his family now? Adrenaline surged through his body. "This is such bullshit!" he bellowed; fists clenched. He stood so fast the chair clattered to the floor. Melissa's eyes widened with surprise.

Melissa sniffed and wiped her nose with the sleeve of her shirt. "What are we going to do?" Her whimper sounded more like a child than a grown woman. It broke him. He wished he could assure her they would get through this, but he felt no such certainty.

They flinched when the sliding door opened. Lucy walked in, Homer by her side. She looked at the chair on the floor, then turned to John. "I heard yelling." Her eyes bore into him.

In a flash, Melissa stood and wiped her tears. "Oh, Sweetie, Daddy isn't mad. We were just having a discussion. Everything is fine."

Lucy's lip quivered.

"I bet you're thirsty," Mel said. "I'll get you some orange juice."

John picked up the chair and lifted his daughter onto it. Homer circled a few times and slumped beneath her. Melissa returned with a glass. "Here you go, love bug." Her voice rang with forced cheerfulness.

John cringed at the charade. He looked at his watch. "Ladies, I'm sorry, but as much as I hate to leave you, Daddy has to shower and get to a meeting."

Melissa grabbed his hand. "Don't go," she pleaded anguish in her eyes. "Please."

He could have called the office, explained something important had come up, but he wanted to be anywhere but home. "This meeting is important. I can't miss it." John pulled her into his arms, breathing in the scent of Ivory soap. "We'll be okay."

She stiffened. "How will it be okay, John?"

With Lucy settled in front of Sesame Street, Melissa started on the dishes. She breathed a sigh of relief when John yelled, "See you later," and shut the front door. Pulling a plate from the soapy water, it slipped through her trembling fingers and clattered to the floor. Shards of blue glass spun across the tile. "Dammit!" she yelled.

"Mommy?" Lucy called.

"It's okay, Honey. I broke a dish." Nerves frazzled, she chided herself for having that second cup of coffee. "Please don't come in the kitchen until I clean it up."

Melissa grabbed the broom. She swept pieces of glass, along with bits of cereal and dog hair, into a dustpan. Flicking away tears with the back of her hand, she dumped the mess into the garbage bin. She wanted to scream. What were they going to do? She splashed cold water on her face and walked through the living room with a strained smile. "Mama's going to take a shower."

"K," Lucy said, not taking her eyes from Kermit the Frog.

Melissa closed the bedroom door and headed to the closet. Sliding her clothes to one side, she reached for the olive-green coat that hung in the back. It had belonged to her mother—the only article of clothing Melissa kept after she died. She buried her nose in the tweed and inhaled. The faint scent of rose water lingered in the material, conjuring feelings of longing. Her mom had been a distant presence in her life, suffering from depression for as long as Melissa could remember. She ran the rough woolen fabric over her face, soothed by the scratchy familiarity.

Inside the satin lining was a secret pocket. At least that's how she thought of it as a child. Often complaining of being cold, her mom sat bundled in this coat, staring out the window, a vacant expression on her face. Melissa would climb into her lap and reach inside the pocket to find peppermint candies. As she unwrapped the crackly wrapper, she'd be granted a weak smile. It was a secret pleasure they shared. In those moments, Melissa felt connected to her.

Today, she reached into the pocket and pulled out a pack of Virginia Slims. The whiff of menthol comforted her. Grabbing the Bic lighter, also hidden in the pocket, Melissa hurried to the bathroom. She tapped the bottom of the box until a cigarette popped out, then flicked the spark wheel. Eyes closed, she took a long, deep drag, relief washing over her. Before she exhaled, she slid open the window and blew smoke through the screen. Turning to the mirror, she faced herself. Fine lines appeared at the corners of her eyes. Her fair skin, like a blank canvas, appeared paler than usual, eyelashes barely visible without mascara. She hoisted herself onto the vanity and inhaled. The nicotine coursed through her bloodstream. Her worst nightmare had come true.

Chapter 2

John sat in his car in the office parking lot. Unable to eat breakfast, his stomach now burbled with acid from too much coffee. He pulled a pack of Dentyne gum from the glovebox and popped two into his mouth, hoping to rid the sour taste. The company he worked for specialized in high-quality fixtures for homes and hotels. Years of construction experience landed him an entry-level position after Kevin was born, offering a much-needed benefit package. Fourteen years later John held the role of Senior Buyer. On a typical day, his mind raced with ideas, excited to start on the newest project. Today, he only wondered if anyone had seen the website. He took a deep breath, grabbed his briefcase, and stepped out of the car. Passing the windowed entry, he stole a glance at himself. His face looked tight, creased with worry. He loosened his tie and opened the front door.

Bonnie, the manager's daughter, flipped through an appointment calendar. An algebra book lay open beside it. He'd heard through the office grapevine that she'd been caught smoking pot on the college campus. To keep a closer eye, Gail put her to work three mornings a week. *Just act normal.* John plastered a smile on his face. "Hi Bonnie, how's your morning going?"

She rolled her eyes. "It would be good except for this ridiculous algebra test. I mean, really, when am I ever going to analyze the speed of a boat in still water versus its speed in a current? I'm in college now; I should be learning more important things."

He winked. "Maybe it's to improve your critical thinking skills."

"If only." She reeked of sarcasm.

John followed voices down the hall to the break room. The thought of coffee made him gag, but he wanted to keep up appearances. He stepped into the kitchen area. Three of his coworkers huddled around Karen Wallace's laptop. Karen looked up in surprise, then quickly shut it. "Oh, John, hi!" Her face wore a pained expression. His coworkers did an about-face and walked to the coffeepot. They avoided his eyes. His heart raced. John made the excuse of a phone call and hurried from the room.

Once in the safety of his office, he closed the door. It would have been easier if Raoul or Mike had said, "Hey John, what the fuck are you doing on the sex registry?" Instead, the uncomfortable silence unnerved him. He toyed with the idea of calling a meeting to address the issue head-on but wasn't sure how many of his coworkers knew about him. He didn't want to alert those who didn't. His hand shook when he reached for the phone and dialed his sponsor's number. Paul answered on the second ring. "My friend, it's good to hear from you."

"Are you free today?" John blurted. "Can we meet for lunch?" Sweat trickled down the side of his neck. He tugged at his shirt. "On second thought, I can't eat. Can we meet at Hanns?" In John's early days of sobriety, he and Paul often frequented Hanns Park. The beautiful lake and hiking trails had a soothing effect on his nerves.

"Umm, sure." Paul sounded confused. "Let's see, it's nine-thirty now. I have a couple of case files to get out. Can we meet at noon?"

"Sounds good. Thank you."

"Is everything okay?"

John's eyes welled up at the concern in Paul's voice. "Everything's fucked. I'll tell you when I see you." He hung up the phone.

It would take him an hour to get to Vallejo, which meant he had to leave by eleven. Two hours to kill. Footsteps echoed past his office. The weekly meeting had completely slipped his mind. John wiped the sweat from his brow and stepped into the hallway. His coworkers fell silent when he entered the conference room. John nodded an awkward greeting. In a swift motion, everyone turned and flipped through their paperwork. He grabbed a seat next to Simon from accounting. Baseball was about the only thing the two had in common. John cleared his throat. "Hey, did you see Cabrera score that tying run last weekend?"

"Yep. It was something." Simon turned back to his notepad.

John feigned enthusiasm as they reviewed the latest textiles. He offered suggestions, but no one commented on his ideas. The room became claustrophobic. It was hard to breathe. I have a dental appointment that I forgot to mention. Getting some work done, so probably won't be back."

Gail, his manager, looked up in surprise. "Oh, okay. Hope it goes well."

It didn't seem like she knew about him. Not yet anyway. John hurried from the room. It would be a matter of time until she found out. He loved his job—needed it. What if Gail fired him? The drive to meet Paul would give him time to think. Once in the car, he inserted *Vivaldi's Four Seasons* into the CD player. The vibrant melodies brought back memories of his dad cooking French toast on Sunday mornings, back when everything was simple.

It had been over twenty years since that camping trip. Now it was back to haunt him.

Chapter 3

1983-1984

John threw his gear into the bed of Kyle's truck. "Damn, I'm stoked for the weekend!"

Richard grabbed the Igloo and hopped into the back seat. "Man, I hear you. Work has been crazy! I barely have time to shit, shower, and shave."

Kyle laughed. "At least you two have a steady cash flow working construction. Since I got laid off from Pay Less, I've been doing stupid-shit jobs—like mowing Mrs. Sowerby's lawn for fuck's sake." He turned the key and revved the engine. "This damn truck eats up my earnings."

"What'd you expect when you bought a top-of-the-line Chevy?" John teased. "You'd pay for it with your good looks?"

"Hell, I can't help it if I've got champagne taste on a beer budget." Kyle put the truck in reverse. "Lake Mendocino, here we come!"

"Can't believe this is our sixth campout since graduating," John said.

"No shit," Kyle agreed. "Brilliant idea to have a Vallejo High campout every Memorial Day. These trips roll around faster every year."

"Time flies when you're having fun!" Richard pulled a pipe

from a small leather pouch and held a baggie of weed to his nose. "This here is some good shit."

"Well then, let's get this party started!" Kyle said.

Richard flicked his lighter and held the flame to the pipe, weed crackling as he inhaled. He passed it to John. "You still sleeping alone these days?"

John took a hit. He held the smoke as long as he could, knowing where this conversation was headed. Finally, he exhaled. "I meet girls, but no one I'm crazy about."

"Q, you need to get laid!" Kyle jumped in, using his nickname from childhood. "If you're still hung up on that Jenny chick, I know the perfect girl to change your mind."

"No, thanks," John grunted. He handed the pipe to Kyle to shut him up. Kyle never had an empty bed. Girls drooled over his surfer's body and sun-bleached hair. Plus, he had a quick smile and personality that made everyone believe he was their best friend. The disc jockey on the radio announced, "Today's date, the twenty-fifth of May, will now be recognized as National Missing Children's Day in honor of Etan Patz who disappeared in 1979." John flipped the stations until he landed on "Let's Dance" by David Bowie. "Lookin' forward to seein' Stan-the-man," he said, changing subjects. "Wonder what he's been up to."

"My brother said he's bringing a woman," Richard said. "I mean a real live divorced-with-kids kind of woman."

"Seriously?" John had a hard time imagining Stan playing the daddy role.

Three grades higher, Stan had strutted around campus like a boss when they were lowly freshmen. He drove a red '67 Mustang and resembled a young Sylvester Stallone. One night in high school, Stan came out of a movie theater with a hot redhead on his arm. John had turned to Richard, and said, "Man, I'd give my left nut to be him for one night!" He still idolized that guy and his natural swag.

"How much beer do we have?" Richard said. "I don't wanna be making any runs once we get settled."

"Relax," Kyle said. "We've got five cases. Should be enough to keep the buzz going all weekend. Speaking of buzz," he flashed a wide smile, "I have a surprise for you losers."

John and Richard looked at each other, then back to Kyle who leaned forward to adjust the volume, egging out the suspense. He looked up with a gleam in his eye. "I scored some 'shrooms."

Two hours later, they pulled into their assigned campsite. Kyle grabbed a six-pack from the ice chest and tossed each a beer. The sound of popping cans filled the air. They gulped, then groaned in unison. "Ahh..."

Richard belched.

Kyle laughed. "Some things never change! Let's get the truck unloaded so we can relax."

High school alumni and their families arrived throughout the afternoon. Former classmates caught up on what they'd been up to the past year. The start of a long weekend filled everyone with excitement. Richard nudged them. "Wow! Do you see what I see?" He gestured to a couple unloading their gear.

The guys stared slack-jawed at the woman standing next to Stan. Denim shorts highlighted her long, tanned legs. A halter top exposed her smooth shoulders. John couldn't take his eyes off the outline of her breasts. Her pointed nipples were visible through the sheer cotton fabric. Two young girls followed close behind.

"Fuck!" Richard exclaimed. "That is definitely a woman."

John grinned and shoved him. "And that is definitely an understatement!"

Stan's arms, loaded with supplies, prevented him from touching her, yet an aura of possessiveness exuded from him. He dropped the supplies and swooped up one of the girls into his arms. John couldn't hear what Stan said, but she giggled. He set her on the ground, giving her braid a gentle tug.

The guys gaped as the mom pulled food and drinks from the cooler, dark hair falling around her toned arms. She leaned across the picnic table, short cutoffs exposing her butt cheeks.

Kyle emitted a low whistle. "God damn!"

"My thoughts exactly," Richard concurred. "Wipe the drool from your chins, boys."

Mesmerized, they didn't notice Stan approaching. "Well, if it ain't the threesome from the hood!" Stan strutted towards them, possessing the same cool he had in high school. The guys jumped up when he offered each a high-five. His biceps bulged with the tattooed letters SAD and Roman Numerals MCMLVI beneath them.

"What's the 'A' stand for?" John asked.

"Antonio." Stan flexed his muscles admiring his physique. "Stanley Antonio DiMarco, 1956, has been hittin' the gym." He looked toward his campsite. "Hey morons, come meet my girls."

They walked toward the picnic table laden with food. John's stomach growled at the spread of bologna sandwiches, Ruffle's potato chips, and orange soda.

"Hey, Babe," Stan said, pulling her from the table. "I wanna introduce you to some guys from the old neighborhood." He wrapped his arm around her waist and turned her toward them as if presenting a prize. "This, my friends, is Angela." His smile widened into a grin at the trophy on his arm.

John couldn't pull his gaze away from Angela's clear blue eyes, so striking against her olive skin. She extended her hand to each of them and made eye contact. John flushed a deep red, stammering like a nerdy schoolboy when he introduced himself.

Kyle flashed a smile, gesturing to the girls. "And who are these beauties?"

"I'm Eliza," the smaller one said. Messy brown curls escaped her long braid. "My sister is Emily. She's six, and I'm four and a half."

Emily peeked out from under thick dark bangs. Her eyes were blue like her mom's. "Hi," she whispered.

"It's very nice to meet you all," Richard said. "I'm sure we'll see you around."

Stan leaned into Angela, kissing her on the mouth. "I gotta go get the rest of our stuff, but I'll be right back." As he turned to leave,

Angela smacked him on the ass with a smirk. "Hey!" he said, pulling her close. They looked into each other's eyes, sexual tension radiating. Embarrassed, John looked away. Stan clapped him on the shoulder and the four of them headed towards the lot.

When they were out of earshot, Kyle turned to Stan. "Man, oh, man, you've got yourself one hell of a woman!"

"Don't I know it!" Stan displayed a shit-eating grin. "Too bad you boys still date teeny boppers."

"Yeah, yeah," John said. "We can't all be cool like you, Stanley."

John took a hit off a joint as chatter from the camp swirled around him. Barbecues emitted a fiery glow—grilled steak wafted through the air. He settled into a camp chair under the backdrop of a full moon. Led Zeppelin's "Stairway to Heaven" sounded from his boombox. He smiled. "This is the life."

Chapter 4

John awoke to the smell of bacon sizzling on camp stoves. Campers bustled about, readying themselves for a day on the water. He unzipped his tent, stepped outside, and wiped the sweat from his brow. "Man, today's gonna be a scorcher! It's gotta be over a hundred already."

Richard pointed to a kettle on the grill. How 'bout a cup of my famous cowboy coffee?"

John opened the ice chest. He grabbed a beer, and a banana, and polished them off in less than a minute. He belched. "No thanks."

In response, Richard bent over and let out a long fart.

"Dude, you're gross," John said, waving the air with his hand.

"No more than you!" Richard said. "Hey, Jones said we can boat with him for part of the day. He's leaving in an hour."

"Sounds good." John couldn't wait to get on the water.

Kyle popped out of his tent, grinning. "Hey, maybe if we're lucky, Angela will come on our boat. Can't wait to see her in a bikini!"

"You dog!" John punched his arm. "Is that all you ever think about?"

"What's wrong with that?" Kyle tossed blond curls from his eyes and winked. "I'm a man who appreciates beauty."

"That you are," John smiled. "That you are."

"Hey, Rich," John said, "toss me another beer." The late afternoon sun beat down on the dock. They'd been on the water all day.

"Sure thing," Richard said. He passed a joint to Kyle.

Kyle took a deep inhale and gestured toward the shore. "Get a load of that!"

Angela, in a bright red string bikini, scooped sand into a pail. Her daughters played alongside her building sandcastles.

"Dude," Richard said, "I can't believe Stan went waterskiing instead of hanging out with THAT."

On cue, Angela bent over in their direction. John blushed at the sight of her firm, round butt. Kyle grabbed his dick, thrusting his hips back and forth. The three burst out laughing.

"Geez, Kyle," John said, "have you no shame?"

"Ha! And you do?" He passed John the joint. "I know exactly what you were thinking when you saw that ass."

"Ditto!" Richard chimed. "I was thinking it myself, boys."

"Hey, Dick," John said, "you're getting red. I think you should slather on more Banana Boat."

"Aww…thanks, Q. You wanna wub some on me?" Richard threw the bottle of sunscreen to John, who tossed it back.

"Rub it yourself, loser."

"But what about my hawd to weach pwaces?" Rich imitated Elmer Fudd when he got stoned.

John grinned. "Maybe Angela will do it for you. Why don't you ask her?"

"Boys, boys," Kyle interrupted. "I think it's time for some magic—as in magic mushrooms." He pulled out a handkerchief and unfolded it with reverence. "Hold out your hands like good little boys and girls. Uncle Kyle's got the goodies."

Kyle deposited the mushrooms into Richard's open palm. Rich immediately popped them into his mouth. He crunched and made a face. "These taste like ass! He gulped the rest of his beer.

"Q?" Kyle offered John the mushrooms.

John hesitated. He was so high already, had been drinking all day. But he didn't want to miss out on the fun. "Sure."

Kyle dropped them into his palm. "Here's to a happy trip!"

John popped them into his mouth trying not to breathe through his nose while he chewed. "Man, these are bad!" He downed his beer and burped.

The logs on the fire crackled and hissed. Sparks ascended into the air. John's gaze followed each one until they disappeared into the night sky. He watched transfixed as campers assembled S'mores, spearing marshmallows onto misshapen sticks. One had to be so attuned to the marshmallow when placing it over the flame. It took only seconds before it turned from a beautiful golden hue that melted perfectly between two graham crackers, to a black, blistered blob erupting into a stringy, sticky mess. He imagined this could be a metaphor for life if he could just figure out how to apply it.

"Hey, Q, you alright?"

John startled when Richard shook him. How long had he been there? Fifteen minutes? Two hours?

His friend peered down at him. "You feel okay? You don't look so good."

John tried to focus on Richard's words, but his friend's mouth made obscene shapes with each pronunciation. John laughed.

"I think you should go lie down," Richard said. "Maybe eat something first, get some food in your stomach. I didn't see you eat any dinner."

John rested his head in his hands. "Naw, I'm not hungry. Maybe I'll go back to the tent and sleep it off." His limbs felt like rubber when he stood.

Richard helped to steady him. "Let me know if you need anything."

John stumbled down the path, ultra-aware of the variations of music echoing from the campsites. Lyrics swirled around his head making him woozy: *There's a little black spot on the sun today, that's my soul up there.* He fell through the opening of his tent onto the sleeping bag. The moment he shut his eyes everything spun. Hoisting himself onto an elbow, John locked eyes on a small stain coloring the canvas. He tried to steady himself. The spot grew and changed, spreading down the side of the tent in a monstrous pool, inching its way toward him. Panicked, he leaped from the tent. Hands resting on his knees, John gulped the cool night air. God, he hated this feeling.

He began to walk, placing one foot in front of the other. The symphonic chirping of crickets reverberated through his head like a well-rehearsed choir. He stopped in his tracks. *Is someone crying?* John craned his ears, but all was silent. He shook his head and turned to go, but there it was again. A whimper. The sound came from Stan and Angela's campsite. They were at the campfire when John left, but he didn't remember seeing the girls. Maybe it was them. John walked to their tent and stopped, wondering if he should get Angela. He'd check first to make sure they were okay. He kneeled and peeked into the flap, steadying himself to keep from falling backward.

The smaller of the girls tossed and turned, emitting low moans. John crawled inside. He put his hand on her back, a feather of a touch. "Shh, it's okay. I'm here now." He lay down beside her. Feeling her warmth through the sleeping bag, he pulled her close. The softness of baby-fine hair brushed against his cheek. He inhaled the sweet scent of roasted marshmallows. It had been a long time since he had slept close to anyone—not since Jenny. A sob rose from deep within. John buried his head in the back of Eliza's neck and drifted off.

"What the fuck are you doing?" A woman's scream pierced the stillness.

John woke with a start, disoriented. He shook his head hard, trying to make sense of his surroundings.

"Stan, help me! He's in the tent with the girls!" Angela pushed him hard, rolling him away from Eliza.

With a yank, Stan grabbed him by the hair and dragged him

from the tent. John yelled in pain. "What's going on?" he slurred. "What happened?"

"What the hell are you doing in their tent?" Stan screamed, spittle flying in John's face. "You some kind of sick pervert?"

"No, no," John mumbled. Distant memories flooded back. He tried to piece them together. "I heard someone crying."

Angela's voice, shrill from hysteria, called to her daughter, "Eliza, did he hurt you?"

"No, Mommy," the little girl sobbed. "Please stop. You're scaring me!"

"Emily, did he touch you? Did you see him do anything to your sister?"

"No, Mama," Emily wailed. "I was sleeping."

John's head throbbed. He covered his ears to block out the sound.

Kyle and Richard stood over him. "What's going on?" Kyle yelled. "What the hell happened?"

"This creep was passed out in our tent, hanging onto Eliza!" Stan's eyes blazed. "Fuckin' pervert!"

"Man, this has gotta be a mistake," Kyle said. "What were you doing in there, Q?"

"She was crying. I came to check. I must have fallen asleep."

"If I find out you touched one of them, I'll fuckin' kill you!" Stan seethed.

John retched. The sour smell of vomit lingered in the air.

"Jesus Christ, the guy is wasted!" Stan said with disgust. "Get him the fuck outta here before I do some real damage!"

Richard and Kyle each grabbed him underneath one arm and dragged him to their campsite. They laid him on a picnic table. "Dude, I don't know what's going on with you," Kyle said, "but this doesn't look good. What the fuck were you doing in their tent?"

"I thought something was wrong," John mumbled. "I went to see." He rolled over and vomited.

"Christ, you need to sleep this off." Richard's voice rang with revulsion. "It will be light in a few hours. We can talk then."

John's head throbbed. The bright sun pierced his eyes like a knife. Richard and Kyle were loading the truck. "I'm sorry, guys. I blew it. I should have gone to get Angela. I'm sober now. I can explain."

Richard turned on him, "They left, John. Too late for explanations. Man, you gotta maintain yourself when you're high." He climbed into the truck and slammed the door. Those in the surrounding campsites stared.

Prickly shame spread up John's neck.

Chapter 5

John stared at the Sports channel, a six-pack of beer by his side. He'd barely moved from the recliner since his return from the camping trip two days ago. No matter how he tried, he couldn't piece together the events of that evening. Bits and pieces came to him, but nothing made sense. The sharp ring of the phone startled him. He muted the TV and picked up the receiver. "Hello?"

"Hey, Q, it's Richard. I got some bad news."

"What is it, Man?"

"I just got a call from Stan. He and Angela took the girls to the emergency room when they left. They wanted them checked out. Stan said Eliza showed signs of molestation."

"Wait, what?" John broke into a sweat. "What do you mean?"

"They said you molested her."

"What the fuck? I would never do anything like that! You know me, Richard!" His breath came in quick gasps. "I would never hurt anybody, especially a kid. That's crazy!"

"I hear you," Richard said, "but Angela is pressing charges. You might wanna go down to the police station. Sort it out. The cops will be calling, but it might look better if you showed up in person. At least it will show good will on your part."

"It will have to wait till tomorrow," John slurred. "I'm in no condition to drive."

"Yeah, right." Richard's tone was one he didn't recognize. Angry?

Before he could respond, the phone clicked. He looked at the receiver, then heard the dial tone. Richard had hung up on him. *Molested?* A growing dread crept over him. What if nobody believed him?

John showed up at work the next day but couldn't concentrate. His legs quavered atop the scaffolding. Afraid he would lose his balance he told his boss he didn't feel well and left for home. He walked through the door and the red light on his answering machine pulsated, taunting him. His hand shook when he pushed the button. A stern male voice boomed into the silence.

"This is Officer O'Donnell of the Vallejo police department. I'm calling to speak to John Quisenberry. I can be reached at..."

John shook when he stepped into the shower. The scalding hot water burned like shame. An hour later, he entered the police station. He stood in front of the information window. "May I help you?" The clerk pushed up her thick wire-rimmed glasses.

John wiped his palms onto his slacks. "Uh, hi. My, my name is uh, John Qui-Quisenberry." The stutter in his voice betrayed his nerves. "I received a message from, um, Officer O'Donnell. I'm here, uh, to speak with him."

"Is he expecting you?"

"Not really, but I came as soon as I got his message."

She motioned to a pair of black couches overlooking the parking lot. "Have a seat. I'll check to see if he's available."

Too antsy to sit, John paced back and forth in front of the window until a door buzzed.

"Mr. Quisenberry? Officer O'Donnell will see you. Please step this way." She pointed down the hallway. "Third office on the left."

John knocked on the open door before stepping inside. He offered his hand to the man behind the desk. "Hello Sir, my name is John Quisenberry. I got your message but planned to come in anyway, to clear things up."

Officer O'Donnell gave John's hand a sturdy shake. He leaned back in a chair that emitted a loud squeak. The buttons on his dress shirt strained against a bloated stomach. "Thank you for coming in Mr. Quisenberry. Please have a seat. I'd like to ask you some questions."

"You can call me John."

The officer glared. A menacing five-o-clock shadow darkened his jowly face.

"Sir," he added.

"John, I have a report here that says you were involved in the alleged molestation of a child. The girl's mother, Angela Stevenson, filed a complaint on behalf of her daughter Eliza. Maybe you can tell me what happened."

John pressed his legs together to keep them from jiggling. He forced himself to remain calm as he recounted the story. He explained that what began as a concern for her daughter, turned into a big fiasco when he was found the tent.

"If you were so worried, why didn't you get the girl's mother?"

John didn't want to admit he was high and didn't think he'd make it back to the campfire. "I didn't want to bother her if nothing was wrong."

"So, you thought it was a better idea to get inside a tent with two young girls?"

John cringed. He saw where this was going.

"Were you under the influence of drugs or alcohol?"

"I had been drinking that day." John didn't want to confess to illegal drug use, which in that moment, scared him more than the molestation charge.

"The girls were taken to the emergency room upon leaving Lake Mendocino. There were indications the youngest had been violated. You claim you fell asleep next to Eliza. You don't remember anything else until the mother's boyfriend pulled you from the tent?"

He nodded. "Yes, sir."

According to Ms. Stevenson, her daughter's nightgown was

bunched around her neck. You had your arms around her. Her panties were askew."

John leaped from his chair. "That's a lie! That never happened!"

Officer O'Donnell threw him a look of disgust. "Mr. Quisenberry, I hereby place you under arrest for the molestation of Eliza Stevenson."

John barely registered the words as his rights were read. He hadn't thought to ask for an attorney before he spoke. The handcuffs clicked around his wrists. A dizzying blackness descended upon him. The officer yanked him hard, and he was led out the door. Fingerprinted and photographed, a guard placed him in a jail cell. John lay on a cot, not bothering to put the folded sheets over the stained mattress. The room darkened, but fluorescent lights from the corridor cast an eerie glow across the room. He checked his wrist for the time, but his watch had been confiscated. The smell of urine wafted up from the corner toilet. When could he make his one phone call? He'd seen that in cop shows.

"Knock it off motherfucker!" A voice down the hall echoed.

"Up yours!" came the reply.

John buried his face into a pillow smelling of disinfectant. He sobbed until he drifted into a fitful sleep.

"Quisenberry!" a voice barked.

John hopped from his cot. "Yes, sir!" He wiped the sleep from his eyes.

"Come with me." John followed the security guard who escorted him to the clerk's office. A woman in a drab green dress handed him a clipboard with forms attached. As if reading from a script, she explained that he would be released on his own recognizance and told him to sign the highlighted areas.

"What am I agreeing to?"

"The judge determined you are not a flight risk," she explained. "No past record, longtime resident in the community, actively employed. Plus, you came in voluntarily without a warrant.

All this worked in your favor." She gave him a tight smile. "These forms are a written formality, promising you'll show up for future court appearances. Bond money isn't required, but all other aspects of your bail remain the same; you may not leave the county before your arraignment hearing, nor engage in illegal activity. The hearing is scheduled for 11:00 a.m. next Thursday. The evidence presented will determine if a molestation charge will be granted. If you don't show up on your court date, a warrant will be issued for your arrest."

John glanced at the papers and signed. He couldn't digest all she was saying and just wanted to go home.

Chapter 6

John forced himself out of bed every morning that week. The sleepless nights were adding up. His effort to get to work on time and appear as if nothing was wrong, put him on edge. Today he snapped at one of his coworkers for dropping a box of shingles. "Dude, watch what you're doing!"

"What's your problem?" Jake spat. "You've been acting like a jerk all week."

John bristled. "Just trying to do my job, which is more than I can say for you!" Fists clenched, he turned and walked away. The moment he got home, he popped a beer. He drank until he passed out, but sleep did not bring relief.

He's on a boat with Rich and Kyle. They're racing through waves in the dead of night. He tosses side to side, unable to get his balance. The boat picks up speed. A huge rock looms ahead. He screams. Crawling on his hands and knees, he propels himself forward. He's got to take the wheel but can't reach it. Help! Someone, help! The boat heads straight for the rock! No, no, no!

The temperature soared to a sweltering one hundred degrees on the day of his arraignment. He wished he had someone with him for support. He'd left messages for Kyle and Richard recounting his notorious night in jail, but neither returned his call. He stood before the judge, sweat trickling down his temples. "Mr. Quisenberry, you have been accused of the molestation of Eliza Stevens, a child under the age of fourteen. Charges include inappropriate fondling and vaginal penetration."

"That's not true!" he blurted. His head whirred in disbelief.

The judge shot a look meant to silence him. "If you do not have the means to hire an attorney, one will be appointed to you at no cost. Do you understand?"

Shocked at the accusation, John couldn't find his voice.

"Do you understand?" the judge repeated.

John gave a slight nod. "Yes."

"How do you wish to plea?"

"Not guilty, Your Honor."

Peering over black-framed glasses, the judge continued, "Mr. Quisenberry, because the court does not believe you to be a flight risk you will be released until your next scheduled court date. During that time, I strongly suggest you obtain legal counsel." The gavel banged in dismissal.

John followed the bailiff to the clerk's office. His signature on the dotted line promised he would report back in mid-September. This had turned into a nightmare. He couldn't do it on his own—that he knew. As much as he hated to, he'd have to ask his parents for help.

Chapter 7

Helen opened the door before John got to the porch. "Well, this is a nice surprise," she said. "I'm so happy you called! I just put an apple pie in the oven." She studied him. "Is everything okay? You look peaked." She brushed a strand of hair from his forehead.

A lump rose in John's throat. "I'm okay," he mustered, "but I have something important to talk to you guys about."

"Uh-oh." His mom frowned. "Are you having girl troubles? Is it your job?"

"Nothing like that. I'll tell you over dinner."

"Well, come in and sit down. Your father will be up any minute."

John's parents lived in the house they purchased as newlyweds. His dad took over the basement bedroom after John moved out, building wall-to-wall shelves to house his collection of 78 records, and 45's. Most evenings he listened to old jazz tunes while nursing a snifter of brandy. The music drifting from the basement stopped.

"Here he comes now," she said.

Henry appeared and patted John on the back. "Hello, Son, how are you doing? Work going well?"

"Yeah," John said. "Work is great."

Helen ushered them to the back patio where she'd set a picnic table with floral dishes and colorful napkins. She carried a bottle of Blue Nun wine and three chilled glasses. John preferred beer, but his mom liked the tradition of wine with dinner. After pouring each a glass, she sat down next to her husband. "Henry, John wants to talk with us about something."

His dad shot him a questioning look.

John gulped his wine. "I've been accused of something. Something crazy. I mean, I still can't believe it."

His parents stared.

"I went on the Vallejo High camping trip with Rich and Kyle. I told you I was going, right? Stan was there—remember Stan from school?"

"I remember Stan," his mom said cautiously.

"His girlfriend has two daughters—they were there too, in the campsite across from us. I wasn't feeling good that night—it was really hot, and we'd been out on the water all day, so I went to my tent to lay down." The words tumbled out. "I heard someone crying so got up to look around. It was coming from their tent, or I mean the tent the kids were in. I checked on them to make sure they were okay. One was crying so I talked to her. I must have fallen asleep, or, I mean, I did fall asleep. They accused me of molesting her."

John stopped to take a breath. The look of horror on his parents' faces filled him with shame.

Helen cleared her throat. "Well, surely no one will believe you did such a thing. Isn't that right, Dear?" She looked to her husband for reassurance.

Henry stared into his wine glass, swirling the liquid. When he did look up, John couldn't mistake the disappointment in his eyes. "Had you been drinking?" John heard the accusation in his tone.

He hung his head. "Yeah."

"Look at me!" Henry's jaw clenched. "How could you have gotten yourself into such a precarious situation?"

John shrank at the escalation of his voice. "I don't know Dad, I'm sorry."

His mom held up her hands. "Let's everyone calm down so we can think this through."

"Helen!" His father snapped. "This is a serious allegation."

"Yes, it is, but pointing out the things he shouldn't have done is not going to help."

Henry let out a long breath. He shifted his gaze to John, who couldn't bear to meet his eyes. "You'll need a good attorney who specializes in cases like this. I'll make some calls tomorrow."

John fought back tears. "Thank you. I appreciate your support."

"Oh, Honey," his mom said. "We'll get through this." She attempted a smile, but apprehension shown in her tear-brimmed eyes.

Chapter 8

John couldn't believe this was really happening. He sat with his parents in the waiting room of the law office. His dad found an attorney who specialized in sex crimes and scheduled the consultation. Henry's leg jiggled next to John, his knee bumping the leg of John's chair. His mom grabbed a Sunset magazine from the coffee table and perused through the pages. John wanted to be anywhere but here. The attorney stepped into the room, and the three of them stood. "Mr. and Mrs. Quisenberry, John, I'm Daniel Laughlin."

Mr. Laughlin had a neatly trimmed goatee and wore an impeccable navy suit. John felt a wave of relief at his commanding presence. Maybe this guy could fix everything. The attorney turned to his parents. "I'd like to speak with your son first, then have you join us. Please help yourself to water or tea."

John followed him into an office the size of a conference room. Mr. Laughlin gestured to a chair. "Have a seat. Would you like some water?"

John's throat was dry. "Yes, please."

The attorney filled a glass from the dispenser and handed it to John before taking a seat at his desk. A huge picture window behind him overlooked the city. He picked up a legal pad. "I understand we're here to discuss an accusation of child molestation."

"Yes, sir."

"You can call me Daniel. I've reviewed the court records and would like you to walk me through the day's events leading up to the alleged assault."

"I'll do my best, but some of the details are fuzzy."

"Fuzzy how?"

John stared at his hands, nervous, afraid of how much to disclose.

Daniel must have sensed his ambivalence. "John, everything you tell me is confidential. I'm here to build the best defense case possible. It's imperative you tell me everything you can remember."

John swallowed. "We partied a lot that day, so I was pretty high."

Daniel scribbled on the paper. "Who were you with?"

"My best friends, Kyle and Richard."

"You were with them the whole day?"

"Yeah, we were camping. There were other people I knew, but I mostly hung out with them. We shared a campsite."

"What had you ingested leading up to the incident?"

"Um, we started with beer in the morning, and then smoked some weed when we got on the boat. I probably would have been okay, but my friend Kyle brought mushrooms. By the time we got back to camp, I was tripping. Then a guy brought out some coke, so I did a couple lines. That's when I started feeling nauseous. I went back to my tent to sleep it off, but when I laid down, I got dizzy."

"Go on," Daniel prodded.

"I thought I could walk it off, you know? And that's when I heard something. At first, I thought maybe it was an animal, but when I stopped to listen, I could tell it was a person."

"What did you hear?"

"It sounded like crying. I walked towards the sound and ended up at the campsite where our friends Stan and Angela were staying. Well, Angela isn't a friend, but Stan is. *Was*, he reminded himself. They were at the bonfire when I left, but the girls weren't there, so

I thought it must be one of them." He reached for his water and gulped. "Someone in the tent was definitely upset. I should have gone to get Angela, but the way I felt, the thought of walking back to the group…well, I figured I'd check on them first. I only looked in the tent to make sure everything was okay."

"And what did you see?"

"One of the girls was tossing and turning like she was sick or having a bad dream."

"What happened next?"

John's heart pounded in his ears. "I went inside." The decision now felt like a boulder on his chest, threatening to crush him. "The one who was crying, I rubbed her back and told her she would be okay and laid down next to her."

Daniel shuffled through the file. "This would be Eliza?"

John nodded.

"How did she respond?"

"She stopped fussing. I think she felt better I was there."

"Did you touch her in any way that could be considered inappropriate?"

"No. I would never do anything like that."

"How long did you stay?"

"I fell asleep. The next thing I remember is Stan yanking me out of the tent."

Daniel didn't show any expression as his pen scratched across the surface of the yellow paper. "Any history of blackouts?"

John picked at his cuticles. "I wouldn't call them blackouts," he said, "but there've been times I drank too much and couldn't remember things." He regretted the words as soon as he spoke, panicked the court could use it against him. What if they said he did horrible things to Eliza and just forgot?

"John, if you've experienced blackouts, it doesn't make you guilty, but it could offer an explanation as to why you don't remember the details."

Beads of sweat trickled down the side of John's face.

"Could you give me some examples?" Daniel said.

John didn't want to incriminate himself further, but what choice did he have? "I got my wisdom teeth pulled in high school and got a prescription for Vicodin. Kyle and Richard, the friends I went camping with, came over with a bottle of Old Crow. I had just taken my pills. I knew I wasn't supposed to drink but did anyway. I threw up on the bathroom floor, but don't remember much else. They said I tried to call 9-1-1, insisted I was dying. They pinned me down and forced the phone outta my hand."

Daniel nodded. "Was anyone hurt?"

"Kyle said I took a swing at him but missed." John chuckled.

"Any other times that you're aware of?"

Aware of. John awoke many times in bed wearing his clothes from the day before. He had no recollection of driving himself home from the bar. But when he drank alone at home, how would he know if he blacked out?

"John?" Daniel prompted. "Were there other times?"

Memories flooded back to that last night with Jenny. He shuddered at what an ass he'd been. His face burned with heat. "There's one other time I know of."

Daniel sat back in his chair. "Tell me about it."

"Two years ago, I went to San Luis Obispo to see my girlfriend. She was away at college. She'd stopped returning my calls, so I drove there to find out why. I was drunk when I showed up at her apartment."

"What happened?"

John had pounded on the door yelling for Jenny to come out and face him. When her roommate opened it a crack, he demanded to know Jenny's whereabouts. He could still recall the fear in the girl's eyes.

"She wasn't there. Her roommate told me where to find her."

"Go on," Daniel said.

John had gone straight to the bar and ordered two shots of tequila. He downed them with salt and lime. His MJM Construction shirt had a big rip in the sleeve and his jeans were filthy. People stared.

"When I got there, the place was packed, a dive bar. Jenny didn't even like country music, but she was line dancing with some guy."

"What happened next?" Daniel held his gaze.

He flashed to Jenny dancing in that short skirt, hair tossed back, laughing. The guy had his hands on her. John had slammed his glass on the counter and stormed onto the dance floor. He would never forget Jenny's shocked expression, the surprised looks on people's faces. Then the guy stood up to him in a threatening way.

"John?"

"I made a scene and punched the guy."

"Then what?"

John had woken up the next morning and staggered out of bed in need of water. His jeans and sheets stank of urine. Rushing to the kitchen, he had vomited into the sink.

"I don't know. Honestly. I woke up at home wearing the same clothes I had on the day before.

"Did you talk to Jenny after that?" Daniel asked.

"She left messages, told me how I embarrassed her, that I was lucky the bouncer kicked me out before Doug killed me. 'Don't ever contact me again!' That's what her last message said. I tried to call her back, wanted to explain, but she wouldn't pick up. I never talked to her after that." It pained him to recall the revulsion in Jenny's voice.

"You don't remember being escorted from the bar?"

"Nope."

"How did you get home? I mean, it's a four-hour drive from SLO."

"I don't know."

Daniel put down his pad of paper. "I'd like to discuss your options. Is it okay for your parents to join us?

John shrugged. He hated to expose them to this bullshit, but again, what choice did he have?

Chapter 9

T he attorney stood. "Hello, Mr. and Mrs. Quisenberry."
Daniel gestured to the couch. "Please have a seat." He sat
down and picked up the yellow legal pad. "John provided
an account of what took place the night in question. I have his permission to discuss the case in your presence. First off, I would like
to explain the laws under PC 288(a). The common phrase *child molestation* is technically referred to in the state of California as *lewd
acts with a child under the age of 14.*"

John registered the shock on his mom's face. The words "molestation" hung heavy in the room.

Daniel looked at John. "As with any crime, a PC 288 requires
proof of certain components which the prosecution must provide.
To convict, they must not only provide evidence you touched the
child but also prove you had the intent to sexually arouse or gratify
yourself."

Helen gasped, clutching a hankie to her mouth.

Daniel hopped up and filled a glass of water. She reached for it
and gulped. He rested a hand on her shoulder. "I'm sorry Mrs. Quisenberry. I know these details aren't easy. Would you prefer to wait
outside?"

"I'll be okay," she whispered. "Please go on."

John stole a look at his dad whose lips pursed in disapproval. He shrank in his seat like a child.

Daniel sat back in his chair and studied them. "I have reviewed the reports, and in my professional opinion, there isn't enough evidence to prove without a doubt that molestation, with intent, took place. If we take this case to trial, I suggest you obtain character witness statements to be used in court to support a *not-guilty* plea."

"What are those?" John asked.

"Witness statements are written by friends and family who know you well. Longevity is a plus. Ask them to focus on your positive traits—decency, honesty, integrity, reliability—that sort of thing. Suggest they provide examples of instances when they witnessed your good character."

"Honey," Helen jumped in. "I know Andy would provide a great reference for you. He's talked to me many times about the great work you did with the youth group last summer."

"Church is a good one," Daniel concurred.

"And your boss," Helen said. "Joe gave you a great evaluation. He can write about your honest work ethic—what a good employee you are. And there's Nancy!" His mom's excitement was building. "When she got divorced, you took the boys to games and played catch with them, acting like a real big brother. She'd be happy to write a letter for you. I just know it!"

John hung his head. How would he explain the need for a character reference? He didn't want anyone to know.

"With these kinds of statements," Daniel said, "it will allow the jury to see you in a positive light, cast doubt on what the prosecution is presenting. However, you must understand it's still a gamble."

His mom pulled at the balled-up handkerchief. "What sort of a gamble?"

"It's a common tactic for the prosecution to pile on additional charges as an attempt to extract a plea bargain. Child Protective Services claims there is evidence to prove Eliza was violated. Those details will be recounted to the jury. The average person has extreme bias when it comes to child assault."

"So, what if they don't believe me?" John said.

"If found guilty, you could get twenty-five years to life in prison."

He jumped from his chair. "I can't do that! I didn't do anything!"

"John!" Henry scolded. "Sit."

John sat.

"You do have the option to take a plea bargain," Daniel said. "In your case, the prosecution is going for *Aggravated Sexual Assault of a Child*. The greater the charge, the more appealing it is to take a plea. If you agree to *no contest*, we can expect the charge will be dropped to *Lewd and Lascivious Conduct*. The sentence would be more moderate."

"Like what?" John asked.

"If the judge agrees to the plea, it will consist of fines and extended probation—but no jail time. However, if you give up your right to a trial, you give up the possibility to be found innocent."

What is the reason behind extracting a plea?" Henry asked.

"It saves everyone the time and cost of bringing the case to trial," Daniel said. "Essentially, it's an agreement between the defendant and prosecutor, so everyone can go home at the end of the day."

"What happens if I agree to the lewd one?" John asked.

"It would still be a *Sex Offender* conviction. You'd be required to register your address with the local police department each year. It's a felony that would remain on your record for the rest of your life."

John's heart quickened. "Who would know about it?"

"The registry is a confidential record maintained by the state. It's used to locate offenders if a missing child is reported, or a sex crime committed." The attorney leaned across his desk. He looked John in the eye. "I think you can beat this. The child in question is too young to relay the events with accuracy. With reasonable doubt, it's likely you'd be proven innocent." The room grew still except for a fly buzzing against the window. It banged against the glass over and over.

Daniel stood. "Why don't you take some time to talk this over? Should you choose to hire me, Vivian at the front desk can provide a retainer agreement outlining my terms."

Henry extended his hand. "Thank you for meeting with us, Mr. Laughlin. We would like you to represent John. Can we get back to you in the next couple of days with the direction we would like to take?"

Daniel nodded. "Absolutely."

Nobody said a word as they walked to the car. John climbed into the backseat of his parents' Chevy Impala, just as he had hundreds of times as a kid. It wasn't so long ago they had been responsible for his life, keeping him safe. He slumped and stared out the window, wishing he could start over. His dad looked at him in the rearview mirror in front of John's apartment. "I suggest we sleep on it. Better to talk when our brains are fresh. Sound like a plan?"

John nodded. His voice cracked when he tried to thank them.

Henry held up his hand to silence him. "We'll talk tomorrow."

John unlocked his apartment and headed straight to the fridge. He pulled a beer from the twelve-pack and downed it in three gulps. Grabbing another, he turned on the TV. The responsible thing to do would be to write out the pros and cons, present it to his parents, and show them he gave it some serious thought. He just couldn't wrap his head around either choice. If he took a plea, he'd have to live with a sex offender charge on his record for the rest of his life. What if his boss found out and fired him? As a felon, he might never get reputable employment.

But to stand trial sounded worse. He'd have to ask people for character references to convince a jury he wasn't a pervert. Plus, he'd have to listen to horrible accusations while people stared. Stan would be there with Angela, glaring at him, judging him. After all the humiliation, he could still be found guilty. And if that happened, he'd go to jail. John wanted his parents to make the decision, tell him what to do. *What a pussy.* He grabbed the pack of beer and settled back on the couch, drifting into an unsettled sleep.

He's in the back seat of the station wagon. The car picks up speed, heading for a cliff. He panics. Neither of his parents is driving! He climbs from the back seat into the front and tries to take the steering wheel. The seat belt is latched, pinning him down. He can't unlock it! He lets out a piercing scream as the car sails over the cliff.

John shot from the couch drenched in sweat. Empty beer cans littered the coffee table. He turned off the TV and undressed. The lights outside his apartment cast eerie shadows through his bedroom window. Sleep eluded him.

Chapter 10

Think about it, Mom," John said. "You want me to ask Andy to vouch that I'm not a child molester? Aren't you worried about the congregation finding out? Dad's a deacon! You really want this public?"

Helen frowned.

John continued. "How can I tell Joe I'm facing a prison sentence without losing my job? I'm scared, Mom. I don't want people to know. Once this gets out, I won't be able to show my face anywhere. You think Nancy will ever let me near her sons if she knows what I'm accused of?"

His mother's pained expression told him she might see the logic in his argument. "Henry, what do you think?"

"John, there isn't anything more I would like than for you to be proven innocent by a jury. Daniel thinks he can make that happen. And I trust his judgment. I'm also fearful that if the trial doesn't go as planned, you could be looking at jail time. Your mother and I will support whatever decision you make, but this is your life we're talking about. The course of action is yours alone.

John struggled to keep back tears, his voice a croak. "I don't think I can go to trial, Dad. The thought of people finding out makes me sick to my stomach. At least if I take the plea, nobody will know.

I mean, who cares if my name is on some list?

Henry moved to the couch and put an arm on his shoulder. Sandwiched between his parents, John wept.

John called Daniel the following day. His attorney's confidence had done little to alleviate his aversion to standing trial. Settling the matter out of court provided a level of anonymity that even his parents thought would give him a better chance at moving forward. "I'll take the plea."

"I respect your decision," Daniel said, "but want to be very clear with you. Taking a plea bargain is admitting to guilt, if only to a lesser charge. You'll be required to register as a sex offender for the rest of your life."

John's stomach lurched. "But you said nobody would know. Right?"

"As I mentioned during our meeting, nobody is privy to this information except law officials. However, if someone called with a specific concern, the police department could release any information they have in your file. Provided you don't give anyone a reason to dig into your past, this will be kept private."

"I can't go to jail." John's voice cracked. "I'm only twenty-four."

There was a pause. "I appreciate your candor. I'll do everything I can."

"So, what's the next step?" John asked.

"I'll put together a case of voluntary intoxication. The drugs you ingested before the event will be cited. This will highlight the fact you were not in the right state of mind, nor in control of your actions.

John was confused. "You'll admit I was on drugs?"

"Yes, and you'll need to check yourself into a rehabilitation center to support the claim that addiction is the root cause, not sexual intent."

"Wait," John blurted. "I have to go to rehab?"

"As soon as possible. Your voluntary admittance provides evidence that you accept full responsibility for your actions. To be offered a plea deal, the persecution needs proof you took the necessary steps to regain control of your life."

John was skeptical. "You think it will work?"

"There is no indication the alleged act was deliberate, nor intentional. I'll argue that your intoxicated state prevented you from forming the criminal intent necessary to commit the crime. Please get to work on securing a spot at a treatment center."

Except for a last-minute cancellation at St. Helena Recovery Center, every rehab facility on John's insurance plan was booked out for several weeks. If he wanted the available bed, he'd have to check-in the following Monday. Four days wasn't much notice to give his boss, but he didn't have a choice. He caught Joe in his office early the next morning before the crew arrived. His boss looked at him over the top of his glasses. "Have you got a minute?" John wondered if Joe heard the tremor in his voice.

"Have a seat," Joe said. "What can I do for you?"

"I know this is short notice, and I want to start by saying how much I value this company."

"Sounds like a resignation. What…you found another job?"

"No, nothing like that." John took a deep breath, willing himself to get the words out. "The truth is I have a problem with alcohol."

Joe removed his glasses and pushed aside his ledger. He leaned back in the chair, granting John his full attention. "I see."

"I'm scheduled to check into a rehab facility on Monday, and well, it's for twenty-eight days. I understand if you don't want me to come back." His words sped up, tumbling out of his mouth, "But I intend to return as soon as I'm out. I'll do an even better job than I'm doing now. I understand if that's not a possibility, given the short notice and all."

Joe seemed to weigh his words. "I once had a problem with alcohol. It cost me my marriage and my home. I'm proud of you for taking this step while you're young enough to avoid the mistakes I made."

John winced. *If he only knew.*

"Your job will be waiting. You're one of the hardest workers I've had the pleasure to employ."

Filled with relief, John thanked him.

Chapter 11

Helen surveyed the expansive grounds of St. Helena. The tranquil mountainside facility overlooked beautiful Napa Valley. "Well, this is really something!"

John's parents dropped him off since he wouldn't have use of his truck. He grabbed his bags from the station wagon and set them on the ground. John faced them. "Thank you for taking me."

His mom pulled him into a hug. "We'll see you on Family Day. Just do what you're supposed to do, and time will fly by. I read in the brochure they have chefs who prepare your meals." She clicked her tongue. "Imagine that!"

Henry shook John's hand and patted him on the back. "Make the most of your time here, Son. May this be a good lesson for you."

John watched his parents drive away. It reminded him of being dropped off at summer camp back in the day. He picked up his bags and headed through the entrance.

The obnoxious schedule began with a 7 a.m. wakeup call and continued throughout the day: 8:30 breakfast, 9:30 individual counseling, 11:00 group therapy, lunch at noon, 2:00 free time, 3:00 alternative therapies, 4:00 fitness, 6:00 dinner, recovery meetings until 9:00, and lights out at 10:00. John struggled with the rigid routine. He wasn't used to accounting for every moment, and desperately wanted a beer at the end of the day. To combat his craving, he lifted weights until his muscles ached.

Once he completed that first week, John kind of looked forward to the group therapy sessions. He grew to care for people whose stories were different than his, yet similar. Plus, he couldn't remember the last time he slept so soundly. Maybe when he was a kid? He woke up refreshed and grew stronger from weight training. The days sped by.

"Is AA For You? Twelve Questions Only You Can Answer." John passed by the pamphlets dozens of times. One night his curiosity got the best of him. It surprised him how many of his answers were "yes". He drank alone. He thought it was normal to come home from work and pop a few beers to unwind. He'd suffered complete memory loss on more than one occasion. He frequently drank to escape worries and often felt remorse the next day. Now his parents had a financial burden due to his drunken behavior. It hit close to home.

Family Day fell on the fourth of July. John sat with his parents at a picnic table where other families gathered. Visiting teens tossed a Frisbee, while Neil Diamond's "Coming to America" sounded from a nearby boombox. Helen unpacked a cooler filled with snacks he enjoyed as a child: Capri Sun, Oreos, string cheese, and Jolly Ranchers. She patted his arm "Comfort food."

A lump rose in John's throat at his mom's kindness, yet the heat of embarrassment crept up his neck. She still saw him as a kid. He gave her a quick hug. "Thanks."

"My, it's beautiful here!" she exclaimed. "I guess if you have to do rehab, this would be the place to do it."

John had waited for this opening. His heart sped up. "You know, when I first got here, I didn't know what to expect, other than I'd probably hate it." He laughed, nervous. "Turns out I've made some good friends. I've enjoyed being here."

"Glad to hear it, Son," Henry said. "Sometimes it helps to take a break from our daily routine to gain perspective."

"I've learned a lot about myself," John continued. His face grew hot, struggling to get the words out. "I believe I am an alcoholic."

Helen raised an eyebrow. "Really? I know you had trouble overdoing it from time to time, but what if you just cut back?"

"I can't manage my drinking, Mom. Cutting back wouldn't work for me. When I leave here, I plan to stay sober. I'll attend meetings and hang out with different people. This program has been a turning point for me. I'm ready to change my life."

"What about Kyle and Richard?" Helen asked. "Won't they be disappointed to lose you as a pal?"

"I haven't heard from them," John said. "Once I got into trouble, they didn't want anything to do with me. And that's probably a good thing. All we did was party anyway."

"Can you still have wine when you come to dinner?" she asked.

"No, Mom. I won't be drinking anything. From here on out I plan to stay sober. There's an Al Anon class at three o'clock I'd like you guys to attend."

"If you want us to go to some kind of class, we will," Henry said, "but I don't see the relevance. If you don't want to drink, fine."

"But it might help if you understand the disease, it's—"

"It's not a disease," Henry scolded. "Everyone drinks at your age. What you need is discipline to know when you've had enough. It's called self-restraint, my boy.

John squirmed while waiting for the meeting to begin. Although he appreciated his parents coming that day, he now had an upset stomach. Doubts gnawed at him over Henry's remarks. The look of disappointment in his father's eyes, and the insinuation that John wasn't strong enough to manage his drinking, really bothered him. *I guess I could just limit myself to two beers.*

His gaze shifted to the man who entered the room. Tall and broad-shouldered, John watched as he greeted staff and patients alike. He looked to be in his mid-thirties. The skin around his blue eyes crinkled when he smiled. Moving to the front of the room, he stood before the crowd. "Hi everyone. Welcome. Some of you know me, but for those who don't, my name is Paul. I'm an alcoholic.

"Hi Paul," the crowd greeted him.

"The reason I show up each month to facilitate this meeting isn't because I expect you to gain anything from the words I impart. Maybe you will, maybe you won't. That, my friends, is up to you. I come because I must share my story, to never forget what brought me to AA."

John leaned forward his interest piqued.

"In 1973, I was twenty-five years old. I drank too much at a local bar, stumbled into my truck, and attempted to drive home. I ran a red light and plowed into a car carrying a family of four on their way home from vacation. No one died, but I seriously injured a little girl." Paul reached for his glass of water and took a sip. "She was only six at the time. It's my fault she'll never walk again." His voice cracked, "Her life will forever be spent in a wheelchair because of me."

Empathetic tears sprang to John's eyes.

"I ruined the life of another human being because I didn't think twice about getting behind the wheel of a car when I could barely walk." A hush fell over the room. Paul wiped tears from his eyes. John couldn't recall seeing a man like Paul, rugged and confident, openly share such emotion. "I recently celebrated ten years of sobriety."

The crowd cheered.

"I'd like to believe that every day I resist the urge to drink, is an apology to the family whose lives I damaged. If I never drink again, it still wouldn't be enough to take back the pain I caused. So, I show up to help others like me and maybe prevent another tragedy from happening. I'll be hanging around after the meeting if anyone wants to talk."

Paul's story resonated with John on a deep level. He wanted to know more about him. It took strength to stand in front of a group of people and share something so personal. What if his dad was wrong about alcoholics being weak? He waited until the crowd thinned before approaching him. He shook Paul's hand. "Hi, I'm John."

"Nice to meet you, John."

"Your story really impacted me. I got myself into trouble with drugs and alcohol and that's why I'm here. I'm in the middle of a legal challenge, and well…I'm scared."

"When do you leave this place?" Paul asked.

"I'll be out next week."

"Do you have a sponsor lined up?"

"I don't. I wasn't sure I needed one."

Paul looked him in the eye and smiled. "Yep, I've been there myself."

John gazed at his feet, searching for the right words. "After hearing you speak tonight, I realize I want what you have."

"What's that?"

"A clean life. A past I've made peace with. A future I'm proud of."

Paul reached into his pocket and gave John his card. "Here, take this. Call me when you're out. Maybe we can get coffee and talk about plans for your future."

"I will," John said. "Thank you."

Paul turned to leave, but John reached for his arm. "Would you be interested in being my sponsor?" His mouth went dry as he waited for Paul's response. He hadn't been this nervous since he asked Jenny on a date.

"I'd be happy to."

John's final few days provoked a feeling of anxiety. The rigorous routine he'd initially resisted provided a renewed sense of energy. A heavy fog had lifted from his brain. Thoughts of going back to his real life unnerved him. John didn't know how to be outside of this facility. He had counted the days until he could leave, but now wished he could stay longer.

His friend, Reggie, approached him in the cafeteria and clapped him on the back. "Hey, you're almost outta here. I'll miss your stupid jokes in group." Reggie walked with a limp, dragging his left foot behind him. His reddish afro couldn't be tamed by the bandana around his head. Blue suspenders held up his pants.

John pulled him into a bear hug. "I'll miss you too, Big Guy." He imagined the jokes and rude comments Rich and Kyle would make about the people John now called friends. It shamed him to know that before his stay, he would have participated in their cruelty. John didn't want to go back to shallow friendships, not after experiencing the solid connections he'd made. Yet remaining sober for the rest of his life seemed unrealistic. Within the safety of this facility, he knew he could do it. He just wasn't convinced he'd be successful on the outside.

John glanced around the room before the commencement ceremony began. It was a little embarrassing that his parents would come all this way to watch him graduate from rehab. He spotted his mom and she grinned and waved like he'd accomplished something great. John didn't see eye-to-eye with his dad, but the man always showed up. The graduates walked to the front of the room and formed an inner and outer circle. They faced one another. Moving in opposite directions, John met each person's eyes and held their gaze, recognizing the bond they shared. He'd always remember this moment.

Chapter 12

J ohn sat across from his attorney. Thrust back into the real world and the legalities of his case disoriented him. He missed the spaciousness of long days caring for his physical and emotional health.

"Are you with me?" Daniel asked.

John shook his head and tried to focus. "Um, yes."

"It's important to continue with AA meetings. I also recommend you find a counselor who specializes in drug and alcohol addiction. Every bit of documentation showing your commitment to recovery will bode well in your defense."

John's mood spiraled by the second. "Okay."

"There's another thing," Daniel said. "The prosecution demands you undergo a psychiatric evaluation."

He tensed. "What does that involve?"

"A psychiatrist will administer a battery of tests. The main one is the Minnesota Multiphasic Personality Inventory test, also known as the MMPI. You'll answer a series of true/false questions, three hundred and thirty-eight to be exact. Once the test is analyzed, the doctor will submit a written report to the court. The prosecution is looking for any indication the results point to pedophilia, versus someone who has committed a sex offense against a child."

John's head whirled. "I don't know the difference, but I'm neither of those things."

Daniel leaned back in his chair, clicking his pen open and shut. "To clarify, a pedophile has recurrent, sexually arousing fantasies or sexual urges involving children. A sex offender has committed an illegal sexual act which involves a child, but who is not necessarily a pedophile."

Daniel must have sensed his bewilderment because he leaned forward and looked him in the eye. "John, we're trying to prove you're not innately attracted to children. And therefore, not a risk to the community. You decided on a plea bargain, which means you forfeited the right for a jury to find you innocent. The best-case scenario is that the psychiatrist's evaluation comes back inconclusive of pedophilia, and the judge grants a reduced plea for *Lewd and Lascivious Conduct*. Our defense is to assert that you did not commit the act with the intent to sexually arouse or gratify yourself, or the minor. But let's be clear, you are admitting to a sex offense. Remember, the goal is to keep you out of jail."

The words sounded foreign; *lewd, lascivious, pedophile, sex offender*. These terms would be used to describe him when he stood before a judge.

Daniel stopped talking. "Are you okay? It looks like I've lost you. Would you like a drink of water?"

John shook his head, wiping away tears. "I'm okay. I just, I don't know. It's creepy that people will think I'm such a lowlife—a pervert. It's bullshit! I'll never move on from this."

Daniel paused before he responded. "This is probably the biggest challenge you'll ever face. You're young. You can rebuild your life. One day you'll look back on this as a bad nightmare. I'm here to guide you through the process as best I can. Shall I continue?"

John blinked hard, quelling tears. "Go on."

"I've chosen a doctor from the court's approved list whom I've worked with in the past. I find him honest and forthright. His name is Stuart Biagi—an expert in the field. I suggest you book an appointment with him. He's not cheap, and it's on your dime." Daniel handed John a business card. "Please take care of this as soon as possible. I want plenty of time to go over the results before the hearing."

John stood. "Thank you."

Outside, John felt as heavy as the hot, humid air. During the treatment program, every slight accomplishment was celebrated. The atmosphere of support gave him hope. Now he faced an uphill battle that seemed insurmountable. Before reaching his truck, he caught sight of a Quik-Stop on the corner. His mouth salivated at the thought of a beer. *Just one. One beer won't hurt.* His feet seemed to have a mind of their own, walking him into the store. Eyes darting over the aisles, John looked to see if he recognized anyone. What if he got caught and blew up his court case? He could go to jail. He hurried from the store, shutting himself inside a phone booth. Breathless, he pulled Paul's card from his wallet and dropped two dimes in the slot. "Please pick up, please pick up."

"Hello?"

He broke down at the familiar voice. "Paul, it's John, from St. Helena. Are you free?"

"Absolutely, Buddy. Tell me where you are."

John stayed inside the phone booth until Paul pulled up. They drove to Hann's Park; a place Paul went to clear his head. They walked along a wooded trail while John explained the legal ramifications of the molestation charge. He hadn't told anyone at St. Helena. Paul pointed to a bench camouflaged by shrubbery, beneath a tree. He motioned for John to follow. When they rounded the bend, a glistening lake came into view.

"I spent hours on this bench staring at the water," Paul said. I sat through sunrises and sunsets, willing myself to find a reason to live." He rested a hand on John's shoulder. "You're going through a rough time. I get how scary it is. It's hard to believe that things will work out amidst this pain, but I give you my word, you'll find value and purpose on the other side. Get up each day, put one foot in front of the other, and have faith in the process."

John held onto his words like a lifeline. Sharing his story with another man who didn't judge him, eased the knot in his stomach. They spent the next hour talking about life outside of AA, sports, and plans they had for the weekend. He breathed easier.

"Let's check in over the next few days and get together Saturday," Paul said. Will that work?"

"Yep, that works," John said. "I look forward to it."

Chapter 13

F ollow me, please." A perky blonde receptionist ushered John into a quiet room. She handed him a questionnaire. "As you know, you are taking the Minnesota Multiphasic Personality Inventory Test, also known as the MMPI. You'll have ninety minutes to complete the questions. When time is up, I'll collect the data, and escort you to Dr. Biagi's office. Any questions?"

John shook his head.

"If you need anything, press the buzzer."

John watched nervously as she shut the door. The small room made him claustrophobic. *What if I fail?* Cracking his knuckles one by one, he shook his hands and grabbed the pencil. *Just answer the questions. I'm not a pervert.*

He quickly scanned the page before starting. The true/false questions appeared benign: "My hands and feet are usually warm enough," and "I am easily awakened by noise." They could be trick questions meant to uncover some deep dark secrets. Unable to crack the code, he answered each one as best he could and finished before the allotted time. He buzzed the receptionist.

She escorted him to an office where a silver-haired man sat behind a desk. Dr. Biagi appeared to be in his mid-sixties and sported a red bowtie. John thought of Pee-Wee Herman, relieving his sense of trepidation. "Come in, John. Have a seat." Dr. Biagi chuckled. "I know being trapped in that room isn't any fun. I hope you had a chance to use the restroom and get something to drink."

"I did, Sir. Thank you."

"You can call me Stuart, or Stu for short. I'd like you to feel as comfortable as if we're merely having a conversation."

"Okay, Doctor—I mean Stu."

"Let's start with your childhood. Seems the most interesting things happen when we are young. How would you describe the family you grew up with?"

"Well, I'm an only child. My mom and dad are normal, I guess. At least as normal as my friends' parents. I played Little League, did okay in school, and we took a trip every summer to Yosemite. Dad didn't like to camp, so we stayed in a cabin which he said was just as good."

"How would you describe your parents' marriage?"

John hadn't considered this before. "Well, Dad went to work every day. He's an accountant, and Mom stayed home doing house-hold stuff. She was pretty involved with church and still is. Dad's a deacon, but it's mostly her thing. I think he does it to make her happy. They get along for the most part, I mean, as far as I can tell."

"Who was the disciplinarian?" he asked. "If there was one."

"Definitely my dad. He liked things a certain way and would get mad when I made a mess or broke something. Mom always stuck up for me. Sometimes they argued she was too lenient. It was tough being the only kid, the sole focus of their attention."

"Did you feel loved?"

"Umm, yeah, I did. I knew my dad loved me. He just didn't show it as easily as my mom— still doesn't. I guess I never meas-ured up to his expectations, even though I wasn't sure what they were."

As Dr. Biagi took notes, John questioned his responses. *Maybe I shouldn't have said that about Dad. Did I make it sound like he was mean?*

"Have you had romantic relationships?"

John began to sweat. This was where he had to show he was a normal guy. "Umm, I hung out with some girls in high school, but I didn't have a real girlfriend until after I graduated.

"Were you sexually active?"

His face burned. He wasn't used to talking about his sex life with anyone but his friends. Certainly not some old guy. "Yeah."

"How was the experience for you?"

John stared at his lap, too embarrassed to meet the psychiatrist's eyes. "It was good."

"How long were you involved?"

"Almost two years. We met at Solano Community College." His voice dropped an octave. "But then she transferred to Cal Poly and found someone else."

"How did you feel about that?

"I wanted to kill the guy."

"But not her?"

"I was pissed at her for cheating on me, yeah." His fists clenched recalling that night at the bar. "But it was him I wanted to take out."

"Are you attracted to young girls?

John's stomach lurched. Here it was. "How young?" he asked. "I mean developed or undeveloped?"

Dr. Biagi leaned back in his chair. "You tell me."

"Well, if I'm walking behind a girl, and she has a nice body, trust me, I notice. But if she turns around, and she's like fourteen, then no. Of course not. Even though her body caught my attention, I wouldn't be attracted to a teenager."

"Do you wear women's lingerie?"

"What? Like pantyhose and shit?" John laughed. "Hell, no."

Dr. Biagi brought out some pictures he called the Rorschach inkblot test. He asked John to report the first thing that came to mind when he viewed each print.

"Uh, that one looks like the Incredible Hulk," he responded when showed a card with black splatter. For another, he said, "Animals in a field with a spaceship hovering overhead."

They spent the afternoon talking about his recovery and the friendships he'd developed while in rehab. John shared his fears of being out in the world without the safety net of St. Helena and expressed his gratitude for having met Paul. By the time the appointment was over, John felt like he had been talking to a friend rather than a shrink.

"Thank you for coming in today, John. I've enjoyed meeting you. Your attorney will receive a copy of my analysis once my report is complete."

The reminder of why he was there caused his throat to constrict.

Two days before the hearing, John arrived at Daniel's office. He sat across from the attorney, hands pressed under his thighs to still their shaking. The attorney grabbed a file from his desk. "I'd like to go over the reports that will be submitted to the judge." He rustled through some pages. "To be expected, there is conflicting evidence. The medical professional who examined Eliza the night of the incident stated that her vaginal area showed signs of trauma, leading him to believe she was molested."

"Bullshit!" John blurted.

"Please let me finish," Daniel said.

John put his head in his hands and took deep, heaving breaths.

"The expert we hired to review the examiner's report suggested that trauma to the subject's genital area could have happened before she arrived at Lake Mendocino or possibly earlier that day. He could not say with certainty that you were responsible." Daniel pulled a page from the file and read it aloud. "It would not be unusual for a child to irritate herself while sitting in sand and water for an extended period. It could explain her discomfort the night the accused found her crying."

"Who will the judge believe?"

"It's not that simple." Daniel tossed the file on his desk. He leaned back in his chair, his brow furrowed. "A physical examination is important, but the diagnosis of child sexual abuse is largely based on the victim's description of the event."

He froze. "Did they talk to her?"

"They did. A child of Eliza's age typically doesn't have the language skills to verbalize an experience of this nature. However, the statement she gave is admissible in court. The prosecution provided a video clip of Eliza playing in her therapist's office, while the psychologist questioned her."

John's throat tightened. "What did she say?"

Daniel pulled a document from the same file and read:

Psychologist: Do you know the person who came into your tent?
Subject: He was my mommy's friend from camping.
Psychologist: Do you know his name?
Subject: I can't remember.
Psychologist: Why did he come in your tent?
Subject: I think because I was crying.
Psychologist: Do you remember why you were crying?
Subject: I didn't feel good.
Psychology: What happened when he came in?
Subject: He rubbed my hair and my back.
Psychologist: Anything else you remember?
Subject: He patted my bottom very gently.
Psychologist: Were you afraid?
Subject: No, I was sleeping.

The attorney put the paper down. "The judge will review this video in addition to the evidence the prosecution is presenting. He will announce his decision at the hearing."

"Is that everything?"

"Dr. Biagi concluded you showed no distinguishable signs of pedophilia, abnormal behavior, or personality disorder. I'm confident a *Lewd and Lascivious Conduct* plea will be granted.

John breathed a sigh of relief.

The attorney stood. "I'll see you in court.

Chapter 14

Dark and overcast, the biting cold December morning reflected John's bleak mood. He shivered in front of the brick courthouse while waiting for his parents. The station wagon pulled into the parking lot, and he watched them approach. They were bundled in heavy jackets and scarves, his mom wearing a knit hat pulled over her ears. He hated dragging them out of the house on such a shitty day. They should be home in their bathrobes drinking coffee and watching "Good Morning America" with David Hartman. John greeted them with a hug. "Thanks for being here. I'm sorry you had to come out on such a nasty morning."

"Oh, don't you worry about us," his mom assured him. Her breath turned to steam. "We're a lot tougher than we look!"

Henry placed a hand on his shoulder, then looked away. "We better head in."

Scanning the courtroom, John spotted Daniel sitting at a table in front of the judge. He conversed with a man in a suit. He guessed it was the other attorney. Angela and Stan sat in the second row with both girls. Eliza spotted him and waved shyly. John looked around to see if anyone noticed, but Angela snatched her hand and whispered something in her ear. The little girl put down her head and stared at the doll in her lap. Stan gave him a scathing look before John turned away.

The judge called his name. Both he and Daniel stood. With trembling legs, John made his way to the attorney's side. "Mr. Quisenberry," the judge said, "I understand you are willing to plead *No Contest* to the charge of *Lewd and Lascivious Conduct with a Child under the age of 14*. Is this correct?"

John's heart beat wildly. "Yes, Your Honor."

"I've considered all the documentation, including this being your first offense. You've never had so much as a speeding ticket as far as I can tell. Therefore, I will accept your plea. However, if you break any terms of your probation, or if any charges are brought against you in the future, the punishment will be severe."

"Yes, Your Honor," he croaked. "I understand."

"I hereby sentence you to a twenty-five hundred dollar fine payable to the court. You are required to reside in a sober living environment for one year. You must register as a sex offender under the state's guidelines for the remainder of your life. The terms of your five-year probation are as follows…" The judge read through each item, but John barely heard a word beyond the fact he wasn't going to jail. His mom exhaled a loud sigh of relief.

Outside the courthouse, John raised his face to the cold drizzle. Daniel approached and suggested they meet in his office to talk in private. "I'll expect you in ten minutes," he said to John.

"May we come too?" Helen asked.

"That's up to John," Daniel said, "but it's fine by me."

John nodded to his parents. He appreciated their support.

They drove separately and reconvened at the law office. The attorney handed John a copy of the court documents mapping out the next five years of his life. "Please follow along while I go through each item. Stop me if you have questions."

The relief John felt after leaving the courthouse left him.

"You have one week from today to move into the Villa, a sober living house appointed by the court. You are not to leave the house except for work or to attend meetings." Daniel smirked. "This encourages residents to attend lots of meetings rather than hang out at the house with a bunch of guys."

"What about Christmas?" Helen inquired. "Surely he can come home for the holidays?"

Daniel turned to John. "You'll have to work that out with the onsite supervisor, but your release time will be hours, not days."

"Oh dear," Helen sighed.

"Your probation will continue for the remaining four years after your release from the Villa. The probation officer assigned to your case will set up weekly appointments to administer a drug test and check on the progress of your meetings. In addition, your PO can make surprise visits to the Villa to administer a breathalyzer or urine test. Once you move out, the PO can come to your residence and your place of employment. If you have one dirty test, John, it breaks the terms of your probation. You'd be looking at jail time. I can't stress how important it is for you to stay clean."

John nodded. "Got it."

"In addition to daily AA meetings and counseling, as dictated by the court, you are responsible for payment of any therapy sessions that Eliza may incur. Each year within one week of your birthday, you must report to the local police station to verify your current address for the database. You could be called in for questioning if a sex crime is reported in your area."

Henry jumped in. "Only law officials have access to the names?"

"Correct," Daniel said. "However, let's say a mother has suspicions about someone in the neighborhood acting funny around her kid. She can call the police department to find out if the suspect has a record, and request information about past crimes. In other words, there must be a pertinent reason to release this type of data. The state doesn't want vigilantism. In addition," Daniel's face was somber, "you aren't allowed to reside within one thousand feet of a school, park, or childcare center."

The heaviness in the air made it hard to breathe. John glanced at his parents. His mom's jowls drooped. What a piece of shit he turned out to be. His face heated with shame. They thanked Daniel for his time and left the building. Rain poured down as they hurried to their cars. The heavy drops mixed with John's tears.

65

Chapter 15

John moved everything from his apartment into his parents' garage—the sum of his life in two truckloads. He hugged them goodbye, then headed twenty miles west to his new home. The Villa turned out to be a dilapidated structure next to the railroad tracks, surrounded by boarded up buildings covered in graffiti. After driving by a second time, John realized the building was indeed the halfway house he'd been assigned. With a sick feeling in his stomach, he pulled his truck into the designated parking area adjacent to a gravel pit. He read the sign: "Smoke 'em if ya got 'em."

John knocked on the front door. He shifted from side to side, surveying the weathered patio furniture. Dried potted plants scattered across the yard. Seconds ticked by. Reaching for the doorknob, he found it wasn't locked. He grabbed his duffel bag and crept inside. Blinds covered the windows, giving the room a shadowy hue. Despite the outside smoking area, the place reeked of cigarettes. "Hello?" he called.

A giant bearded man wearing a worn flannel shirt poked his head around the corner. "I'm Allan, the house supervisor. What can I do for you?"

"Um, I'm John Quisenberry?" It came out more like a question. "I'm here to check in."

Scratching his stomach with both hands, the guy looked him up and down. "Not what I expected," he said, "but this place takes all kinds."

John didn't know how to respond.

"The house is empty right now," Allan said. "Guys are at their meetings but give it another hour and you won't feel so lonely." He chuckled.

"Uh, where should I put my stuff?"

The man gestured with a beefy tattooed arm. "At the end of the hall. You're bunking with Geraldo."

John walked through a crowded room, past dingy couches and a stained recliner with cotton poking out. A small television with rabbit-ear antennas sat on top of a bookcase. Pamphlets on addiction, religion, and life-after-parole stacked the shelves. A fake Christmas tree sat on a card table in the corner of the room, it's only decoration a strand of lights with three blinking bulbs. Stunned by the degradation of his life, he trudged down the hall to find his room.

The Villa's residents were either on parole or awaiting court dates. Except for recovery meetings and those lucky enough to have employment, the men were sequestered to the house twenty-four hours a day. Eight people inhabited four bedrooms, each containing twin beds and two small dressers. The two bathrooms were a free-for-all, used by everyone. John got up early the following morning to make sure he got to work on time. He stood outside one of the locked bathrooms checking his watch every couple of minutes. Pacing back and forth he hesitated, then knocked.

"Whataya want?" a voice boomed. "I'm on the can!"

"Uh, sorry," John said. "I have to be at work by seven."

"Fuck off," came the reply.

John jumped in his truck and stopped at the nearest gas station. He peed and splashed cold water on his face. Using wet hands, he slicked down his hair. Fighting back tears, he raced to work.

Aside from his job, he attended AA meetings and went for coffee afterward with other recovering addicts. "Fellowship" they called it. The men were open about their personal lives and emotional struggles—a sharp contrast to the conversations he'd had with Kyle and Richard about who got laid and where to score weed. Paul showed up every week to work on the twelve steps with him. The first step: recognizing his powerlessness over alcohol, was something John came to terms with while in rehab. He struggled with the second step: finding faith in a power greater than himself. His parents raised him to believe in a God with whom he had no relationship.

"You know," Paul said, "it's okay to create your own understanding of a higher power."

"Like what?" John asked.

"Have you ever been somewhere, or spent time doing something that brought you peace?

John imagined the stillness he experienced when fishing on the river. "When I'm out in nature, especially near water, I feel like the Universe is so much bigger than me. It kinda makes me believe there's an order to it all, like everything has a purpose. Like, maybe I have a purpose."

Paul grinned. "That, my Man, is your higher power. The next step is to let go of control and trust in that higher power. Turn your life over to that which is greater than you."

When it came time for the fourth step—taking a fearless moral inventory of himself—John admitted that many events in his life triggered resentment. "I don't see the point in revisiting situations I want to put behind me," he complained. "After all, I'm not drinking now."

"Until one understands the patterns in their behavior," Paul said, "you can't address them. It's like peeling back the layers of an onion. Just take them one by one."

Adrenaline pumped through John's body when speaking of the breakup with Jenny—that awful trip to San Luis Obispo. It still pissed him off that she dumped him without the courtesy of a conversation.

Paul rested a hand on his arm. "Try to put yourself in Jenny's shoes. Imagine what it was like for her."

John hadn't been the best boyfriend. He'd criticized her for choosing a college so far away, acting surly when she called to share stories about her classes. Oftentimes he was drunk. He confessed to Paul that he showed up wasted at the bar and acted like an asshole in front of her friends. "I was a real jerk."

"It's important we gain awareness of the parts we played," Paul said, "but imperative to forgive ourselves for not knowing better at the time. Release the shame, or it could lead us right back to the bottle."

"I get it," John said, "but she's the one who cheated on me."

Paul gave him a playful punch. "It takes time, my friend."

Chapter 16

Bridges to Recovery was a meeting the court mandated John to attend. He despised it. The group was comprised of women who had been sexually abused, and men who were convicted perpetrators. Facilitated by a therapist named Kelli, the setting provided space for open dialogue to promote healing between the victims and perps. Many of the women had been molested as children, often by a family member or someone they trusted. Others were raped or violated in a perverse way. Some expressed an inability to find trust in the intimate relationships they so desperately craved. Others acted inappropriately or were overtly sexual. All of them carried lifetime scars.

The men, brutally honest, talked about fighting inappropriate feelings for children. Others viewed their abnormality as a disease. Some had physically and sexually battered women they claimed to love. John witnessed rough looking men weep as they apologized for the damage they'd caused. Never had John abused a woman. Except for some dirty movies in high school, he'd seldom watched porn. The fact he had to be in a room with men who committed these types of crimes, disgusted him.

Last night a woman turned towards him. "I'm so sick of men like you, sitting there acting like you wanna be anywhere else." Her dark eyes blazed with fury.

John looked over his shoulder to see who she was speaking to, but there was nobody behind him. Dumbfounded, he said, "Um, excuse me?"

"There's no excuse for a man who assaults women and children," she snapped.

John's face burned when he realized all eyes were on him. "It wasn't like that with me. I—"

"Bullshit! You're all the same. Think you're entitled to take anything you want just because you can."

The therapist jumped in. "Lynn, I hear how frustrated you are when you believe perpetrators don't take responsibility for their actions. Would you like to use the pillow?"

John didn't know what Kelli was talking about, but the woman nodded.

The facilitator brought over a big cushion and placed it on an empty chair in front of Lynn. She sobbed, punched, and kicked, shouting profanities. Burying her face in the center, she howled like a wounded animal. Her screams so primal, the hair on his arms stood up.

God, he needed a drink.

"Hey Quisenberry!" The house supervisor yelled from the kitchen. "Phone!"

John didn't receive many calls, so hurried to the telephone. "Hello?"

"Hey, it's Paul. I'd like to personally congratulate you on your first year of sobriety."

"Uh, thanks," John said.

"I'm heading over to pick you up and treat you to a burger at Hank's. Are you ready?"

"I just got out of the shower," John said. "But, yeah, I can be ready in ten."

At the diner, John's AA buddies surprised him with a store-bought cake. A single candle stood in a mound of frosting that read,

Congratulations John! The group sang, "For He's a Jolly Good Fellow". Heat rose to his face.

"Make a wish before you blow out the candle," Paul said.

John only wanted one thing—to make it through the next six months and get the hell out of the Villa. He took a breath and blew out the candle.

His friend Dylan nudged him and winked. "Hey bro, you're free to date now."

John laughed out loud. He'd noticed girls at meetings, but the program recommended not getting involved with anyone until after a year of sobriety.

John raised an eyebrow. "In due time, my friend, in due time."

Chapter 17

Audrey facilitated a Saturday AA meeting that John attended. The first time he heard her speak, she captivated him with her dark humor.

"So, there I was crashed out on the stoop of this apartment building," she said, "surrounded by birds pecking at the leftovers in my Taco Bell bag. Their fluttering wings and tiny toenails scratching the paper woke me. I rubbed my eyes and felt something slimy on my fingers. I looked at my hands. Bird poop. I had smeared it on my face. You would think that would've been a wakeup call, passed out, birds shitting on me, but no, I wasn't ready to face the piper yet."

Her audience stared wide-eyed until she laughed, making it okay for others to join in.

"It took losing custody of my daughter before I got my shit together."

The crowd grew quiet.

"I locked her in the car while I ran into a bar for a quick drink. 'Mommy will be right back,' I told her. When the police found me, she'd been in the car alone for two hours. I went to jail and my brother was granted temporary custody. For a mother to lose her own child, well, that's the biggest fuck-up of all." Her tears flowed freely. "When the drugs and alcohol took away what I loved most in the world, I knew the time had come to surrender."

Attracted to Audrey's honesty and zest for life, John began spending time with her outside of AA whenever his schedule allowed. Although six years older, her pixie haircut and big blue eyes gave her a girlish appearance. One night after a meeting, they found themselves alone on a park bench. Audrey scooted into him, took his arm, and placed it around her shoulder. "Ooh, you're nice and warm."

John froze.

"Are you okay? I mean, with this?" She pulled him closer.

"Yeah, sure," his voice cracked. "It's just, I wasn't expecting it." *Idiot!* "I don't think I've been with a woman, sober. I'm not sure I'll be good at it."

She kissed him. "We'll figure it out."

Being with Audrey brought every insecurity to light. No longer an option to rely on a substance to relieve his anxiety, he muddled through their lovemaking like an inexperienced virgin.

"Talk to me," Audrey said. "Tell me what you're feeling."

John buried his face in her neck so she couldn't see him. "Like I'm not satisfying you." His voice shook. "Like you're going to realize you've made a huge mistake and dump me."

"Never," she said. "It takes time to get to know each other's bodies, to figure out what works." She tilted his face to hers. "I'm crazy about you, John. I'm not going anywhere."

Although the program recommended taking it slow, there wasn't anything slow about it. Audrey made him feel like he was okay, worthy of love. It had been so long since John felt the touch of a woman, he couldn't keep from rushing in. Limited to stolen moments, he raced to Audrey's apartment after work or dashed to her place for a quickie following an evening meeting.

"Not joining us for coffee again?" Dylan asked with a wink.

John hurried to his truck. "Nope, not tonight."

Often, he burst through the Villa's front door as the clock struck ten.

"Cutting it a little close there, Buddy." Allan would point to his wristwatch, then crack a smile.

Good behavior and regular meeting attendance earned him extra time on the weekends, enabling him to spend long leisurely hours in Audrey's bed. The two rarely left her apartment until growling stomachs sent them in search of food. They'd been together three months when the court granted Audrey an unsupervised visit with her daughter.

"Gretel's birthday is Saturday," Audrey said. "I plan to take her to the AA picnic at Children's Wonderland. I'd love for you to meet her. Would you like to spend the day with us?"

They were propped up in bed, naked, eating leftover chow mein from a takeout container.

"It starts at one," she continued, "but I'm going to pick her up from my brother early to spend some time with her. I thought we could meet you there."

The room shifted. Sweat accumulated under John's armpits. Audrey knew he was mandated by the court to live at the Villa, but John had never laid out the full story. He'd rehearsed the words in his head, but no matter how he spun it, he knew it could be a game changer.

"Hello?" She nudged him. "Earth to John."

"Audrey, there's something important I need to talk to you about."

She stopped mid-bite, noodles hanging from her chopsticks. "What?" Her tone implied she expected the worst.

John exhaled a long sigh. "The reason I'm at the Villa is because of a molestation charge."

Audrey's eyes widened. She dropped the food back into the container and set it on the nightstand. She stared at him.

"Nothing happened. Honestly. I got really wasted on a camping trip and passed out in a tent where a couple of girls were sleeping. The parents found me, and I was accused of molesting one of them."

Audrey's eyes shone with confusion, but he forced himself to continue.

"I'm so sorry I didn't tell you sooner, but I didn't know where our relationship was headed, and then it got serious. In hindsight, I should have said something earlier, but I wanted to wait until…" John's voice cracked. "I have to register as a sex offender." He wiped the sweat from his forehead. "It turned into a big mess."

Audrey didn't take her eyes off him.

"Say something," he begged. "Please."

Her words came out in a whisper. "I want to ask a question if you promise to be honest."

"Okay."

"Could you have done something?"

John let out a long breath. "I had no business being in a tent with young girls. I get it. I would never hurt anyone, especially a child. But I have no recollection of that night. My attorney insisted I would be found innocent if we went to trial, but I couldn't chance it. If a jury found me guilty, I could have gone to jail. So, I took a plea bargain instead."

Audrey's expression held no clue as to what was going through her head.

"Are you going to say anything?" he pleaded.

She inched her body away from his. "First off, I appreciate you telling me the truth. We all have stories that brought us to recovery. You know the things I've done. Sometimes I make myself sick thinking about them." Tears rolled down her cheeks.

He reached for her hand, but she shook her head.

"I adore you, John. You've been a rock for me these last few months, but my priority is to provide a safe place for Gretel to live. If it were just me, I could put aside anything you might have done, because I know who you are. But it isn't about me. As much as I love you, my focus is my daughter. I've worked hard to comply with everything the court has asked. I'm almost there. I can't—won't—jeopardize my case. If anyone finds out I'm dating a sex offender, well, you must understand the position I'm in."

John stood and grabbed his pants from the floor. Her words

were like a knife to his heart, yet he couldn't be angry with her. "I respect your decision Aud, but I can't pretend I'm okay."

She didn't stop him when he headed for the door.

77

Chapter 18

2004

John arrived an hour early to meet Paul at Hann's Park. Except for an occasional phone call, he and Paul rarely connected. John and Melissa moved from Vallejo soon after they married, and the distance made it difficult to get together. Plus, with three kids, well, he rarely had time to do anything. John thought back to those last weeks at the Villa after Audrey dumped him. Paul showed up daily, dragged him to meetings, and forced him to keep it together. "You're almost out of here," he encouraged. "Life will look a whole lot better on the other side. I promise."

And it had.

John's parents helped him with a down payment on a fixer upper. He'd spent the remaining four years of probation going to work and renovating the house. Most important, he stayed sober. Once he completed every court requirement, John was finally able to breathe again. Then Melissa walked into his life. He met her at a barbecue hosted by a mutual friend and was immediately captivated by her auburn hair and eyes the color of jade. Soon, their easy banter became flirtatious. She offered her phone number, and they quickly became an item. Daily he agonized over how, or when, to bring up his conviction. He'd avoided dating since Audrey, for this very reason. If the relationship were short-lived, he wouldn't have to tell Melissa. Though keeping it from her felt dishonest. The uncertainty clung to him, coloring every conversation they had. One night while cleaning up after dinner, she pulled him close. "I love you, you know."

John had waited too long. He remembered the pit in his stomach. Melissa sensed his unease and pulled away. Holding him at arm's length she looked him in the eye. "If you're having doubts about our relationship, tell me. You've been distant and preoccupied, and I can't help but think you're having second thoughts."

He'd faced her with tear-brimmed eyes. "I don't have any doubts about wanting to spend my life with you, but there is something from my past I haven't told you about. It may change the way you feel about me."

Melissa had paled. "You're scaring me."

The tremendous weight of his secret now equaled the imagined pain of her rejection. He let the awful words tumble out. "Five years ago, a woman accused me of molesting her daughter. It was on a camping trip. I fell asleep in a tent with two girls."

"I don't understand," Melissa said. "Why were you in their tent?"

"They were sisters. One was crying so I sat with her to be sure she was okay. Unfortunately, I fell asleep. I was an idiot. A drunken idiot. When Angela, the mom, checked on the girls, she found me asleep in the tent, next to her. She freaked out and went to the police. They accused me of molesting her."

"But you didn't do it, right?" Her voice shook.

"I patted her back," John said, "stroked her hair, comforted her. I promise you, Mel, I would never hurt a child, but it didn't look good. My attorney recommended we take the case to trial confident I'd be found innocent. But I had been using drugs and blacked out. That would have come out in the hearing. I was scared the prosecution could claim that I didn't remember what I had done. I could have gone to jail. I couldn't risk it."

"What did they say you did?" she asked.

"When Angela took Eliza to the hospital, they reported her vaginal area was irritated."

Melissa covered her mouth in a gasp.

"The doctor suggested that sitting in a wet bathing suit in the sand all day could cause irritation, which could be the reason for her distress. Or something could have happened before the trip. It would have been their word against mine. I took a plea bargain to guarantee I wouldn't go to jail. I was twenty-four, Mel. I needed a guarantee."

"What are the legal implications?" she whispered.

"I have a felony and have to register as a sex offender. I'm not allowed to live within one thousand feet of a school or park, and I can't own a firearm—not that I'd want one in the first place." He chuckled, trying to make light, but the look of horror on her face silenced him. "I know it sounds like I'm the scum of the earth, and if I had to do it over, I'd maybe take my chances and go to trial. Back then, a plea was all I could manage. It was a dark time for me, Melissa."

"What does the police department do with your name?"

"It's a computer database that law enforcement maintains, so if an assault is committed, offenders in the area can be brought in for questioning."

"Can anyone see the names?" she asked.

"It's only available to officials."

"Who knows about this?"

The people involved in prosecuting me, also my parents and sponsor—and a girlfriend I had when I first got sober. Nobody else knows, Melissa."

"Where does this girl live? Is there a chance you'd run into her family?"

"I don't think it's likely. I knew the mom's boyfriend from high school. The last I heard, they all moved to Sacramento."

Her empty expression was worse than if she screamed or threw things. "I wish you would have told me sooner," she whispered.

"I wanted to, but I wasn't sure if we were just dating, or if you saw a future together." John tucked a piece of hair behind her ear. "I understand if it's too much and will understand if you leave tonight and don't look back." He took her face in his hands, wiping the tears with his thumbs. "I'm in love with you, Mel. I'll respect whatever you decide."

She nodded as if in deep contemplation. John pulled her into his arms. He held her close, wondering if it would be the last time.

"Right now, I don't know what to think. I'm blindsided. I don't want to say anything until I've had a chance to absorb it."

Breathing in the scent of her hair, John released her. He watched, holding his breath, as she gathered her purse and sweater. "I'll call when I can." She wouldn't meet his gaze. John stepped outside and watched her drive away. He collapsed onto the porch step. The cold concrete was a stark contrast to the heat of his emotion.

He waited. Two days turned into three, then four. John had walked around in limbo, zombielike, as he did in 1983 awaiting his arraignment. He had all but talked himself into never hearing from her again when the phone startled him awake. Nobody called him late at night, except Melissa when she couldn't sleep. His hand shook when he reached for the receiver. "Hello?"

"Hi, it's me."

At the sound of her voice, John bolted upright. He didn't speak for fear of breaking the spell.

"I don't want more time to pass before we talk," she said. "Can we meet at Joe's on Saturday morning?"

"Sure, sounds great." His throat was dry, making it hard to get the words out. "How about ten?"

"That works," she replied, businesslike.

He lingered, hoping she would say more, but the seconds ticked by. "Okay, see you Saturday," he said.

"Bye, John."

She hung up before he could say goodbye.

John's heart pounded when he saw Melissa through the window. She sat at a table overlooking the courtyard. Her chestnut hair, tied back in a ponytail, accentuated her high cheekbones. God, she was beautiful. He approached her table, struggling to stay calm. "I'm so happy to see you!" he blurted. *Too desperate*, he chastised. His underarms were slick with sweat. He wiped his brow and slid in next to her. "I feel awkward—like it's our first date or something."

The waitress appeared, poised with a pen and pad. "What can I get you started with?"

"Hot chocolate for me, please," Melissa said. "With whipped cream."

The waitress turned to him. "Just coffee for me, thanks."

"Room for cream?"

"No, just black."

"I'll be right back with your drinks."

John wiped his palms on his jeans. He reached for her hand. "Mel," he began, but she cut him off.

"I need to say everything on my mind, so please hear me out."

His hands fell back onto his lap. Drops of sweat beaded on his forehead. He flashed back to when Audrey broke it off with him. He leaned back, preparing for the worst.

Melissa fidgeted, appearing to gather herself. "From the very start, I knew you were different. You're so stable compared to the men I've dated. You have a great job and you've renovated a beautiful house. I admire your commitment to sobriety and the personal work you've done. You are so kind to your parents, and I've grown to love them. I've often imagined Henry and Helen being grandparents to our children."

His heart plummeted, waiting for the word, "but".

The waitress dropped off the drinks and stood ready to take their order. John looked at Melissa, a question in his eyes. Understanding, she nodded.

"Joe's omelet for each of us," he said. "And an order of Belgian waffles to share." The comfortable familiarity carried a pang of grief.

Melissa took a sip of hot chocolate. John reached across the table, and gently wiped a dollop of whipped cream from her nose. She offered a sad smile.

"I'm still shaken by the bombshell you dropped on me," she said. "It's not easy to reconcile that the man I love and trust, is a man convicted of a sex offense."

John's head drooped with shame, imagining the worst.

"I talked it over with my sister. I needed her to help me process it. Donna would never tell me what to do, but she asked a lot of questions to help me gain clarity. She promised to support me whatever I decided."

John's heart pounded like a hammer in his chest. He wanted her to get to the point.

"I don't know what happened that night," she said, "but I keep coming back to the man I know today. The traits I most admire are probably because of what you've been through. It doesn't make sense to embrace those qualities and then suddenly discount them because of what you disclosed."

Relief flooded his pores, yet he wasn't quite sure what she was saying. "Does this mean you can see a future with me?"

"I'm open to the possibility," she said. "I'd like to continue spending time together and see where it goes. It's been a setback, and I'll do my best to move past it. Could you be patient with me?"

He had reached across the table and took her hands, kissing one palm at a time. "Thank you," his voice wavered with emotion. Thank you for giving us a chance."

John believed when they married, the worst was behind them. How naïve he'd been.

Paul pulled up and jumped from his car. He greeted John with a grin. "Look at you!" he exclaimed with a whistle. "I'll never get used to seeing you in a suit. You'll always be that scruffy kid in Levi's."

John slapped his back and hugged him. "Well, some of us have to grow up and get a real job."

Paul laughed, punching his arm with affection. They headed towards the walking trail.

"Seriously, Buddy," John said with sincerity, "you haven't aged one bit in the last twenty years."

"It's all that good living," Paul said with a chuckle. He worked as a counselor at a nonprofit rehabilitation center, helping people transition into sober lifestyles. He never married. "Too many clients are dependent on me," he had joked. "Adding a wife, kids, and dog to the mix, would put me over the edge."

They walked in silence, waiting to speak until further up the path.

"The sex offender registry is online," John said. "It's available to the public. I don't know what to do." The words tumbled out. "Anybody can view my name. It could destroy my life."

"Man, that's tough," Paul said. "I can't even imagine what you're going through."

John kept talking, "I walked into the breakroom today, and everyone was looking at my co-worker's laptop. She shut it down when she saw me. They had to see it—my name."

Paul beckoned to a familiar bench. "Let's sit." The two had often come here before John moved from Vallejo. Whenever either needed support, the other would receive a phone call with the words, "Hey, do you have time to meet at the park?" Code for: "I need to talk."

The two stared at the lake in companionable silence. The sound of water lapping at the shore, normally soothing, did little to calm John's nerves. Paul put his hand on his shoulder. "Man, I don't know what to say. It's so unfair."

"What about my kids?" John said. "What happens when they find out their dad is on a website for perverts? What if their friends find out? Or their parents?"

Paul's voice soothed, "You have nothing to be ashamed of. This is old stuff making its way to the surface. You have every right to hold your head high and act with integrity. You and Melissa have an incredible relationship. You'll find a way to get through this together. It's fucked-up, but your friends know you. It won't change their view. If it does, they weren't your friends to begin with."

John sighed. "I know everything you say is true. But, if it were only me facing the humiliation, I could handle it. I'm worried for Melissa. I don't want her life destroyed because of my past mistakes."

The moments ticked by, neither saying a word.

"I'm here for you, Buddy," Paul assured him. "Are you going to meetings?"

"I haven't been," John admitted. "I'm so busy with work and kids, AA was put on the back burner. It's not like I'm tempted to drink, so I kinda stopped going."

"Yeah, I know you've had it dialed in for some time, but it might be a good idea to pick it back up. It would offer some support."

"Yeah, you're probably right. Let's walk."

Together they meandered through the wooded area. John filled him in on work and the joy of raising teenagers while Paul shared his concerns about possible funding cuts to his program. They circled the lake and ended up at the parking lot. John reached to shake Paul's hand, but Paul pulled him in for a bear hug. "I love you, Brother." He took hold of John's shoulders. "You call me any time. I mean it. You don't have to do this alone."

Tears sprang to John's eyes. He honestly didn't know where he would have ended up without Paul's faith in him. "Thanks, Man, I'll keep in touch."

Chapter 19

Driving home, a sharp ding from the gas gauge startled him. The orange needle hovered over E. Preoccupied, he hadn't noticed the car was close to empty. Pulling into the nearest gas station John inserted his debit card at the pump. While the car fueled, he grabbed his cell phone from the glove box. *One missed call.* John recognized the number from Lucy's school. Why were they calling him and not Melissa? He stared at the voicemail icon. A slow creeping dread took hold of him. He entered his passcode.

"This is Judith Banks, director at Harmony School. I have an important matter I would like to discuss with you. Please call me when you get this message."

John got back in the car, shut the door and slammed the steering wheel. "Fuck!"

It took years for him to pass by a school without looking over his shoulder, let alone feel comfortable participating in his children's activities. The California Penal Code denied sex offenders the right to enter any school building or grounds without written permission from an administrative official. When he hesitated to attend Kevin's first kindergarten play, Melissa argued he couldn't possibly avoid every event. Aware of the legal requirements, he suggested they get permission first.

"Absolutely not!" she exclaimed. "The last thing we want is to bring this to someone's attention. It's not like anybody would suspect you of something."

John showed up that afternoon to Kevin's performance, despite his better judgment. The indiscretion hovered in the back of his mind like a wagging finger. By the time Diana entered kindergarten, he had grown more comfortable making appearances but remained cautious. Never did he walk onto a soccer field or attend a back-to-school night without scanning the crowd to see if he recognized someone aware of his past. The prospect of running into Stan and Angela with the girls terrified him. He envied the seamless way other parents blended in.

Unlike Kevin and Diana, Mel enrolled Lucy in a charter school, which required parent involvement. Melissa helped in the classroom, and John did yardwork on the weekends. Just last week Mel had approached him and said, "Lucy's class is going to Strawberry Farm next week. They'd like as many parents as possible to chaperone."

"That sounds fun," he said. "Lucy will love it. You plan to join them?"

"I thought it would be nice if you came, too."

He'd raised his eyebrows in surprise. "You know I can't, Melissa."

"It's been over twenty years for heaven's sake! Nobody is going to suspect you of anything."

"You don't think I would love to accompany my daughter on a field trip?" Frustration edged his voice. "I hate the fact I can't participate."

"But no one would know," she whined. "It's not like you're on anyone's radar."

"Mel, we've been following the news for months about Megan's Law. It could be published any time. I'm not taking any chances!" It irked him that his wife wanted to pretend this wasn't an issue. "I can't believe you'd even ask." He walked into the bathroom and shut the door.

The voicemail from Lucy's school probably substantiated his worst fear.

The house smelled of disinfectant, alerting him to his wife's stress level. When troubled, Melissa scrubbed the house from top to bottom, trying to create some semblance of order. She kneeled on the floor in front of the coffee table, a can of Pledge in one hand, a white cloth circling the wood surface with the other. The "Talking Heads" blasted from the stereo. She looked up, startled. "You're home early."

John turned down the volume, took the furniture polish and cloth from her, and set them on the table. He pulled her up alongside him. "You've been crying."

She lowered her head to his chest and let out a sob. "I'm so scared! What happens if the kids find out? Or their friends at school? I waved to Kate when I left for the gym, but she gave me a weird look, I mean, it seemed like a weird look, like she knew." Melissa hiccupped. "What if the neighbors don't want us to live here anymore?"

His wife's body quaked against his. Paul's words came to mind. "Mel, our friends know us, know me. I'd like to believe they'd give me the benefit of the doubt." He tipped her chin to look into her eyes. "In any event, no one can make us move. This is our home. We have every right to be here."

"But what if we should move? Maybe go someplace where nobody knows us. I don't want the kids to—"

He put a finger to her lips, shushing her. "It wouldn't matter if we moved. No matter where we go, I'd still have to register my address with the police department. We have to let this play out."

She let out a long sigh. "How did it go at work?"

"It was okay." He wasn't about to tell her he walked in on his coworkers viewing the website. But he did have to tell her about the voicemail. "The director from Lucy's school left a message for me to call her."

"Judith?" Mel stiffened and pulled away. "Why would she call you and not me? Do you think it's about *this*? Call her back."

Melissa's voice was urgent. "Now!"

John kicked himself. He should have called first before telling Mel. A creeping dread spread through his body. Now she'd be privy to their conversation. He pulled out his phone and punched in her number. He prayed the director wouldn't pick up.

"Good afternoon, this is Judith."

Did he imagine her disapproving tone? She must have recognized his number.

"Hi Judith, uh, this is John Quisenberry returning your call." He stammered like a kid sent to the principal's office.

"Thank you for calling back. A certain matter has been brought to my attention that I need to discuss with you. Any chance you can come in tomorrow before Lucy's class?"

"Umm, sure. May I ask what this is regarding?"

"I'd rather discuss it in person."

Fuck. With his wife standing by, he tried to suppress his rising panic.

"Sure," he replied coolly. "If Lucy can stay in the playroom before class, Melissa and I can come tomorrow at noon. Would that work?"

"Actually, this may not be a meeting you want your wife to attend," she said.

His knees weakened. "Judith, there is nothing I will discuss without my wife present."

"Suit yourself. I'll see you tomorrow at twelve."

John pressed the disconnect button. "Such bullshit!" He threw the phone.

Melissa's face crumpled. She flopped on the couch and covered her face. John didn't go to her. Nothing he could say would bring comfort. His inadequacy as a husband sickened him. He headed up the stairs. "I'm going to take a shower."

That night he and Melissa flopped into bed exhausted, but neither slept. John sensed her turmoil as she tossed and turned. He stared at the ceiling, guilt-ridden. Rather than finding comfort in each other's arms, they remained on opposite sides of the bed.

Chapter 20

The following morning John greeted the receptionist, but the pink-haired teenager barely mumbled a hello. Had she purposely avoided eye contact? John sequestered himself in his office until it was time to meet the director at Lucy's school. He tapped Bonnie's desk on the way out and smiled. "Have a good lunch."

She glanced at him from under her bangs. Letting out a puff of air she blew strands of hair from her eyes. "Sure thing," she said.

John smiled. He wouldn't let her sarcasm get to him.

Melissa stood with Lucy in front of the school. His daughter ran to him. "Daddy!"

John swooped her up and kissed her forehead. "You're my best girl!"

He grabbed Melissa's hand and squeezed it. She had bags under her eyes and worry lines creased her forehead. "It'll be okay," he reassured her.

"I hope you're right," she said. Her tone told him she expected the worst.

They signed Lucy into the playroom and walked down the hall. The director's door was ajar, but John knocked out of respect.

Judith stood. She gestured to two chairs. "Come in. Please sit down." She crossed the room and shut the door. Clicking heels on linoleum echoed in the quiet room. Her jet-black hair was cut short in a chic, masculine style, adding to her coolness. John braced himself for the reprimand.

Judith spoke as if reading from a script. "It has been brought to my attention by one of our parents, that your name," she looked directly at him, "is listed on Megan's Law, the sex offender registry." Her gaze shifted to Melissa eyebrows raised. John guessed she was measuring his wife's reaction, wondering if this news surprised her. Melissa stared back, poker-faced. Judith continued. "This information puts the school in a precarious situation, and—"

"Who told you?" Melissa demanded.

"That's not important," she said. "The information is public knowledge, and—"

John cut her off, "Judith, this registry is very misleading. I entered a plea bargain for an alleged offense when I was twenty-four. I was accused of something I didn't do. For God's sake! It was twenty-two years ago!"

Her expression didn't change. "In addition," her blue eyes flashed, "the state of California requires that you inform the school of your conviction, and request permission before coming onto the grounds—which you failed to do. This is a reportable offense."

Melissa started to say something, but Judith held up her hand. "Which I will not do," she added. "I don't wish to cause harm to your family. But I do have a responsibility to keep our parents informed."

"Informed?" Melissa's voice was high-pitched. "So, what are you saying? You're going to send out an announcement in the bulletin?"

Judith shot her a look meant to silence her. "I'm hoping we can come to a mutual agreement. If you want Lucy to stay enrolled it would require that you, John, request written permission from myself and the entire parent body, to approach the school grounds."

"What if I agree not to come near the school?" John said.

"Melissa would be required to fulfill the monthly hours on her own. She'd be solely responsible for drop-offs and pick-ups."

"That's doable," Melissa jumped in.

Now his wife sounded eager, desperate even. It pissed him off.

The director looked at John. "If Lucy has playdates with other children in your home, I must notify the parents of your status."

"That's ridiculous!" John slammed his hand on the desk.

Melissa jumped, but Judith didn't flinch. "Please understand the responsibility this puts on me as overseer of this school. Although I can see you're frustrated, news like this will stop the heart of any parent whose child is enrolled. If something inappropriate happens to a student in your home, and the parents haven't been notified, it would be grounds for a lawsuit. We must take every precaution."

Keeping his voice as steady as possible, John spoke in monotone. "Nothing would ever happen to a child while in our home. Our teenagers have friends over all the time. We have a normal family, Ms. Banks, just like every other parent at this school."

Judith smoothed a piece of hair behind her ear, exposing a diamond stud. "We can't take the risk. If you propose to keep Lucy enrolled, you cannot drive a classmate in your car or have them in your home unless the parents are properly informed ahead of time. I'm very sorry, but a charter school is governed by the parents. I report to them."

"Are you saying a public school doesn't have the same requirements?" Melissa asked. "Of telling the other parents, I mean?"

"Correct," Judith said. "A sex offender must always request permission to come onto the school grounds, but their personal information cannot be released. A confidentiality clause protects parents with criminal records."

Melissa looked at him, her green eyes filled with tears. He put his arm around her and stood. "Thank you for your time, Ms. Banks. We'll let you know what we decide."

Chapter 21

L ucy Goose," Melissa said, "let's go on a walk."

"Okay, Mommy! Let me grab my purse and keys."

Melissa chuckled. Lucy's comment lifted her spirits despite another sleepless night. She had laid awake obsessing over the conversation they'd had with Judith. "Grab your sweater, Honey. It's chilly outside."

Lucy skipped to the front door with Homer close behind.

"Mommy, he wants to come with us." She reached for the leash as the dog raced around her feet. Tiny hands struggled to clip it to his collar. "There we go, big boy," she said. "All set."

The three of them stepped into the cool morning air. Homer trotted and sniffed the ground while Melissa admired the gorgeous colors of changing leaves. They moved to San Mateo when John landed the position at Edward-Morgan Interiors. She loved their house. It was home. What would happen if the neighbors found out?

"Mommy, look!" Lucy pointed to the neighborhood elementary school. "That's where Kevin and Di went."

Melissa timed their walk so the kindergarteners would be at recess. She feigned enthusiasm. "Look at all the kids!"

"They have a really big yard," Lucy said. "Look at the jungle gym and slide."

She took Lucy's hand and walked around the side of the building. They stopped in front of the school's office. "Honey, wait right here with Homer. I'll only be a moment." The smell of freshly waxed floors greeted her. Her heart warmed at the familiar face behind the counter. "Good morning, Edna."

"Why Mrs. Quisenberry, how nice to see you. How are those two youngsters of yours?"

"They're great. Middle school and high school if you can believe it."

"Oh, the kids grow up so fast around here," Edna lamented. "Please say hello to them for me. What can I help you with today?"

"I'd like to pick up a registration packet for our youngest daughter, Lucy. She started kindergarten at a charter school last month, but, well, I'm considering moving her to Baywood."

"Of course, Dear. Let me round up the paperwork."

Melissa knew there was nothing to consider. She couldn't keep Lucy at that school. How could she ever meet the eyes of a parent and not wonder what they thought of her? She imagined their hushed tones whispering, *Poor Melissa! Married to a child molester! Why does she stay with him? If I found out my husband molested a child, I would cut off his balls!* Regardless of what they said about John, Lucy would take the brunt of their family's secret; excluded from birthday parties and play dates at best; and harassed by classmates who overheard their parents discussing it, at worst.

Edna gave her the packet. The secretary knew every child "by smile", as she liked to say. It struck Melissa how opposite she was from Judith. Stepping outside, she took Lucy's hand. "How about we go to the beach today?"

"What about my classes?" she exclaimed.

Her expression, serious and wide-eyed, caused Melissa to laugh out loud. "I think it's okay to miss one day. Let's take advantage of the sunshine. Besides, it's Friday and I'm ready for the weekend."

"Can Homer come?"

Of course, the big guy can come."

Melissa gazed at the beautiful tree-lined street, biting her lip to keep from crying. However unfair, she blamed John for putting them in this predicament. Yes, he'd been honest, but assured her his felony was confidential. Besides, she couldn't have grasped the ferocious love she would one day have for her children. Or her primal instinct to protect them.

A short drive from their house, the family had been coming to Moss Beach for years. Melissa found a shady place against the rocks and spread out a blanket. She slathered Lucy with sunscreen and secured her hat.

"Come on, Homey," Lucy said. "You'll have lots of fun splashing in the waves."

Melissa walked along the ocean's edge, rehearsing the words she would say to her daughter. Lucy splashed and shrieked while Homer frolicked alongside her. She grabbed Melissa's hand, pulling her into the surf. "Come on, Mommy! It's only cold for a second. Your toes get used to it." Like a statue, Melissa grimaced as the ice-cold water rushed over her feet. Homer leaped from the waves and shook water all over her. She screamed and jumped out of his way. Her feet sought the warmth of the sand where she buried her toes.

"My tummy's growling," Lucy said. "I'm a hungry monster!"

Brushing sand from the blanket, Melissa took out peanut butter and jelly sandwiches, potato chips, and two cartons of apple juice. Despite her nerves, she too, was hungry. Halfway through her sandwich, she turned to Lucy. "It was so nice when your brother and sister went to the school down the street. I know you love your kindergarten class, but maybe it's better if you were closer to home."

Lucy looked up, breadcrumbs dusting her lips. "But, why?"

"Well, because Homer and I could walk with you every day."

"But what about my friends at my school?"

"I know you'll miss them, but there are lots of kids from our neighborhood who you'll get to know. When you're bigger, you can even walk home with them."

"Do I have to? What if I want to stay at my real school?"

"I think you should attend the school near our house."

Lucy set down her sandwich. Big tears slid down her cheeks. Melissa thought her heart would break. "Oh, Sweetie." She pulled her close. "I know it isn't what you want, but I promise you'll be happy there." She hoped it would be true.

Lucy fell asleep on the couch when they arrived home, allowing Melissa to call her sister. Four years older, Donna had always been her closest ally. Their father made a career in the U.S. Marines, requiring that the family relocate every two years. Donna never minded moving to a new place, but Melissa didn't have her sister's ease of fitting in wherever she went.

"It's a chance to reinvent yourself," Donna said, responding to Melissa's dread at starting a school year with people she didn't know. "Just think, you're free to change your hairstyle, the clothes you wear, your whole personality—like trying on the girl you wanted to be at the last school."

Melissa had a hard enough time fitting in as herself, let alone trying to be like somebody else. On top of that, their mother became more despondent with every move and could offer little support. At the sound of Donna's voice, Melissa broke down. "It's me," she sobbed.

"Oh, Mel," Donna soothed. "What's going on?"

She relayed the awful meeting with the director of Lucy's school, and Judith's plan to notify the parents of John's status. "We can't keep her there," she cried. "I had to tell her she'd be leaving the school she loves."

"Oh, no. How did she take it?"

"She was so disappointed! I tried to make it sound exciting like it would be fun to walk to school with kids from the neighborhood."

"Children are resilient," Donna said. "She'll make new friends before you know it."

"But now, I'm worried about Kevin and Diana," Melissa said. "With everyone on the computer these days, it's only a matter of time before someone sees the website. What happens if they find out?

"For one thing," Donna said, "nobody is going to randomly scroll through the site, or type John's name into the search engine."

"You can look by zip code, Donna!" Her voice rose an octave. "The name Quisenberry jumps out!"

"John is not convicted of child molestation," Donna said.

"He's convicted of lewd & lascivious conduct involving a child!" she shrieked. "How is that any different than a child molester?"

"Oh Mel, I wish I could help you. I can't even imagine what John is going through. He prides himself on caring for his family, but despite his stoicism, you're the stronger one."

"I don't feel strong," she whimpered.

"Hang in there, Sis. I love you."

Chapter 22

John arrived home after a shitty day at work. His co-workers, Sam and Ollie, walked right past him that morning without a greeting. So obvious was their dismissal he'd called out, "And good morning to you, too!" Later, he passed Sandra's office and saw her whispering on the phone. Spotting him, she hurriedly said, "Goodbye" and hung up. John fumed. The unspoken words tormented him more than anything said out loud.

He opened the front door and with forced cheerfulness, called, "Hello, hello!"

"Daddy!" Lucy jumped into his arms, squeezing her legs around him.

John twirled her. "Did you have fun at school today?"

"I didn't go to school. Me and Mommy went to the beach. It's why I was so tired I needed a nap like when I was little."

Melissa walked into the room. He raised his eyebrows, trying to get a read on her.

Lucy continued, "Mommy told me I had to go to a new school and that didn't make me happy."

John sat her on the couch in front of the TV and walked over to Melissa. "Everything okay?"

She led him into the kitchen. "I couldn't take her to Harmony."

Her eyes welled with tears. "The thought of running into Judith, or parents who might know, well, I couldn't. We took a walk to Baywood. I picked up a registration packet. I think—"

"You think changing schools is best for Lucy?"

"I want her safe, John. We can't wait until the school announces our business in a fucking newsletter!" Her nostrils flared.

"Mommy?" Lucy whined.

Melissa snapped her head around. A look of chagrin crossed her face. "I was just telling Daddy about your new school. I guess I got overly excited."

"But you sounded angry."

"Mommy isn't mad. I just have a lot on my mind." Melissa patted her head. "Can I make you a snack?"

Lucy pulled herself onto the kitchen chair, dragging her blankie behind her.

Melissa set out some cheese and crackers, then turned to him. "I didn't plan anything for dinner. Just order pizza."

The door slammed and Kevin burst into the kitchen. His once-white football uniform was covered in mud stains. Dark sweaty hair stuck to his forehead. The smell of sweat and AXE deodorant emitted from his body. "What's for dinner?"

"It's your lucky day," John said. "Pizza!"

Kevin stripped off his jersey and threw it on the laundry room floor. "Cool. I'm taking a shower."

Diana appeared in her blue and white cheerleading uniform; chestnut hair pulled high in a ponytail. John pulled her in for a hug. "How's my girl?"

"Dad, stop. I'm all sweaty." She laughed and pushed him away. "Call me when it's time to eat."

John slipped into bed, yawned, and pulled the covers to his chin. He closed his eyes and sighed loudly. "I'm beat."

Melissa rested a hand on his shoulder. "John?" she whispered. "We have to tell Kevin and Diana."

His eyes shot open. "Geez, Melissa."

"We can't let them find out at school. It has to come from us."

John couldn't disagree, but it was happening too fast. He wasn't ready to face his children.

Melissa continued. "They have crafting day at the gym tomorrow. Lucy will be there for an hour and a half. Maybe we can pick up sandwiches for lunch and take Kev and Di to the park."

Adrenaline coursed through his body. "What would we tell them?"

"We tell them the truth. That this happened years ago, and you're innocent."

It was hard to speak over the lump in his throat. "What if they hate me?"

"They'll need time to digest it, but they won't hate you. You know that."

John stared at the ceiling, resigned to another sleepless night.

Chapter 23

T he teens sat silently in the car. Two sets of headphones leaked muffled rap beats into the stillness. Claiming they had better things to do, neither wanted to go to the park. They got lunch from the deli and walked across the street to the park. "There's a picnic table," John said, pointing to one in the distance.

No one said a word as they unwrapped their sandwiches. "Hey, you guys," Melissa's tone was gentle, "there's something important we want to talk with you about."

Both kids looked up—worry etched on their faces. John's heart raced.

"Are you getting divorced?" Diana appeared panicked. "Emily's parents just told her that her dad is moving out and they have to sell the house, and move into an apartment, and—"

Melissa touched her arm, quieting her. "No, Honey, it's nothing like that."

"What then?" she challenged.

John watched his wife struggle to respond. She started and stopped as if weighing her words. "When Dad was a young man, he got convicted for a crime he didn't commit. Although it was long ago, it stayed on his record."

"Why are you telling us now?" Kevin asked.

John had allowed Melissa to lead the conversation but now cleared his throat. "A new law requires people convicted of certain crimes to be listed on a website..." He paused, gathering all the strength he could muster, but his voice failed him.

"And your name is on it?" Kevin's eyes widened in amazement. "On the internet?"

John struggled to meet his gaze. He recalled his son's first words, "Like you, Dada", as the toddler imitated his every move.

"Yes." John fought back tears. "My name is on it."

"Can anyone see it?" Diana said.

"It's a public site," Melissa said.

Diana looked puzzled. "What does it say exactly?"

He and Melissa hesitated. They'd agreed ahead of time not to use the term *sex crime* or *sex offender*. "Dad's conviction involves a young girl." Melissa's voice betrayed no evidence of the anxiety that undoubtedly filled her.

"Does it show a picture of you?" Diana asked.

John nodded, praying his children would never see it.

"For real?" Kevin said. "Like a mugshot?"

He winced. "Yep."

"But are you smiling?" Kevin pressed. "In your picture?"

John almost laughed. Only his son would ask this question. "No, Son, I'm not smiling."

"We're telling you now," Melissa interjected, "because you might hear something at school. Dad and I want you to know the truth."

"But what is the truth?" Diana asked. "What is it they say you did, Daddy?"

How long had it been since she'd called him Daddy? He missed the girl who looked at him, eyes filled with adoration. The words he uttered next could change the way she viewed him. "A mom accused me of hurting her daughter." John's face burned. "I was in the wrong place at the wrong time. It was a big misunderstanding. I—"

"But didn't you tell the judge you didn't do it?" Diana interrupted.

"I did, Sweetie, but it wasn't that simple. The judge offered me a deal. If I agreed to take responsibility, I could go home. Otherwise, I might have gone to jail. I know it's confusing, but at the time, I did what I thought best."

Kevin looked baffled. "What does the internet say you did, Dad? To the little girl."

John peered at Melissa, silently pleading with her to take over. He couldn't speak, could barely breathe.

"Dad was accused of touching her inappropriately."

Their children were familiar with this term. Kids as early as preschool were taught the difference between *good touch* and *bad touch*.

"Can't you do something?" Kevin asked. "Like, hire a judge and explain you didn't do it, tell him it was a big mistake?"

"I wish it were that easy, Son, but it's not." His children's eyes clouded. How he wished he could protect them from this horrible truth. "I love you so much," he said. "Your mom and I are so sorry this happened. We wanted you to know the whole story in case you heard something. We didn't want you to be caught off guard." John felt their minds race, but neither spoke. "Do you have anything you'd like to ask me?"

Both shook their heads in unison.

"Mom and I are always here, for anything you'd like to know."

They nodded, but neither looked at him. Hoping to change the subject, he said, "Hey, you want to stop by Best Buy on the way home? They probably have the new *Pirates of the Caribbean* video. Maybe we can have a popcorn and movie night."

"Sure," they mumbled.

Kevin devoured his meatball sandwich, but Diana didn't take one bite. Wrapping it in her napkin, she put it back in the bag. John watched as she walked with her brother, head down, to the trash bin. He turned to Melissa, who seemed a million miles away. "How do you think they took it?"

She gave him a sad shrug. "It will take time to process, but they know we're a team and love them. We do our best to keep their lives as normal as possible."

John stood and pulled her to him, needing to feel the solidness of her body. "Thank you for standing by me."

Her body stiffened. "Do I have a choice?"

Chapter 24

Melissa walked over to Baywood school on Monday morning. Her hand shook when she turned the doorknob to the school's office. Edna greeted her with a warm smile. "Well, hello again."

Melissa put on a brave face. "We decided Lucy should attend the neighborhood school." She handed over the packet.

"Let's have a look-see." The secretary flipped through the pages.

Melissa's eyes drifted to the familiar nametag shaped like an apple, "EDNA" etched in black against the red background. She had worn it for years. Her bright blue sweater stretched over her plump body. It was adorned with appliques of pumpkins and black cats. Edna's graying hair and horn-rimmed glasses added to the whole "Mrs. Doubtfire" look. Melissa understood why the children loved her so.

"Thank you for providing a copy of Lucy's immunization record," Edna said. "You don't know how many parents turn in their packets without one."

"If possible, I'd like her to attend the afternoon session."

"I'm sorry." Edna sounded as if she were disappointed. "The afternoon session is full. It seems to be the preference of parents these days. The morning class runs from 8:30 to 12:00. Can you make that work?"

Melissa preferred having time in the afternoon when all the kids were in school, but it took only a moment to register what a small compromise this would be. "Yes," she nodded, "that will be fine."

"When would Lucy like to start?"

"I hoped it would be today, but since the morning class is already in session, can we plan for tomorrow?"

"Of course, dear," Edna soothed.

Melissa turned and flicked away tears with the back of her hand. "Thank you for your kindness," she blurted out.

"We'll see her tomorrow morning, Mrs. Quisenberry."

Melissa arrived home and peered into the backyard. Lucy served John a pretend meal from her play kitchen. Widening his eyes, he clapped his hands in delight. He was so good with the kids, it was devastating to imagine that people would now look at him with disgust. She picked up the phone and dialed the number for Harmony School. "Hello, Judith. This is Melissa Quisenberry. John and I think it's best for Lucy to a different school."

"I understand," the director said. "The situation is unfortunate, but we must adhere to the law."

"You know the kind of family we are," Melissa croaked. She slammed down the phone, her face hot with humiliation. Putting on a bright smile, she opened the slider door. "Hey, you two, do you have room for one more?"

John recognized her smile as forced, but her face didn't seem as drawn as when she left the house.

"Here's a banana split, Mommy." Lucy gave her a blue dish with a plastic banana.

He squeezed her leg. "Is everything okay?"

She tilted her head from side to side and shrugged.

He kissed her cheek. "Ladies, I hate to leave a date early, but it's time for work." He patted Lucy's head. "Daddy has to make the big bucks so you and Mommy can keep your kitchens stocked."

Melissa stood. "I'll walk in with you."

"See you later, alligator," Lucy giggled.

"In a while, crocodile!" he called back.

Once they were inside, he turned to her. "How did it go?"

"All set for tomorrow morning."

He wrapped his arms around her. "I know you're disappointed, Mel. I'm sorry."

"We were able to put this fire out, John, but how many more will there be?"

Chapter 25

John couldn't shake the sinking feeling in his stomach when he pulled into the office parking lot. Every workday was more uncomfortable than the last. His colleagues seemed to regard him as a specimen under observation—rarely speaking to him unless they had to. He walked through the double glass doors, relieved that Bonnie wasn't at her desk. She had no problem giving him the cold shoulder. Down the hall, he heard her voice from the manager's office, the door slightly ajar. "Mom, how can you let a guy like him work here? I mean, how disgusting is this?"

He stopped in his tracks. Gail spoke in a hushed whisper. He couldn't make out her response.

"I kind of agree with Bonnie," a woman chimed in.

He recognized Beverly's voice, a sales assistant, and good friend of Gail's. "I mean, what if a client finds out that one of our buyers has a record of child abuse? Think of the effect it could have on the clientele we attract. Especially when he represents himself as this all-American guy!" She let out a sarcastic laugh. "What a joke!"

"I've always thought he was a little creepy," Bonnie said, with disgust. "He tries to joke with me when he walks by my desk—like overly friendly."

"Not so loud!" her mom shushed.

John stood paralyzed. He wanted to burst through the door and tell them off. Instead, he hurried to his office before doing something he'd regret. Shutting the door behind him, he leaned against the wall for support. He'd imagined what people might say about him, but his stomach roiled at hearing it firsthand. He picked up the phone and dialed Mel's cell but hung up before it rang. "Fuck!" he swore under his breath. He paced. Could he walk into the office and face them? *I need a drink.* The thought came from somewhere deep inside. He shook his head hard.

Mustering his courage, he headed towards Gail's office. Bonnie, on her way out, strode past him without a word. John tapped on the open door, announcing his presence. Both women looked up in surprise. Gail clicked her keyboard—minimizing the screen, he guessed. "John. Come in. Please."

John stepped inside and shut the door. The strong scent of perfume gagged him. He worked to keep his voice steady. "Gail, Beverly, you obviously saw my name on the registry." He tried to appear calm, but his voice wavered. "I'd like to clarify some things for you."

Both women stared.

"This *thing* is something I was accused of when I was twenty-four. For God's sake! It's ancient history. Regardless of what that damn website says, I'm not a child molester. I took a plea bargain to avoid the publicity. I'm not comfortable going into detail, but I can assure you, I'm not some kind of monster. You know me, Gail."

Beverly looked down at her bright-red manicured nails, as if she didn't want to be part of the conversation.

Gail cleared her throat. "First of all, I want to apologize for the insensitive way I approached this. When Bonnie showed me the site, I admit, it shocked me. You overheard us speaking. I didn't know you had come in. Not an excuse to behave in such an unprofessional manner, but this information caught me off guard."

"I understand." He sank onto her couch.

Beverly rose from her chair and walked to the door. "Excuse me. I'm expecting a phone call." The scent of Chanel No. 5 trailed behind her.

"Honestly, John," Gail continued, "I don't know how to proceed. If word gets out that we have an employee convicted of such a crime..." Her voice trailed off. "Well, I just don't know. I plan to have a conversation with the regional manager about possible liabilities."

John's heart stopped. "You aren't saying I could lose my job?" The life he'd carefully built was crumbling piece by piece.

"Let's not jump to conclusions," she said. "I just found out about this. I'll confirm how to proceed and will keep you apprised. Surely you can understand."

He shot out of the couch. "Gail, I've been a good employee for many years. I trust you have my back." Not giving her a chance to respond, John exited. His anger rose like mercury in a glass thermometer. Once inside his office, he went straight to the computer. He opened Internet Explorer and typed *Megan's Law* into the search engine. Heart pounding, John waited as the page loaded. A search box appeared where a name, address, city, or zip code could be entered. He scrolled through the disclaimer that spelled out the legal uses of the site. It stated the registry could be used for informational purposes only. Harassment of a listed offender was punishable by law.

John typed in his zip code. He figured this is what a random searcher would do to check out a specific area. In the *Radius* box, he clicked *5 miles*. Tapping *enter*, he held his breath. In an instant, the screen populated a map with blue markers targeting the streets of known offenders. More than he'd expected. He changed the search to *2 miles*. The markers decreased dramatically. *Only five!* He wiped the sweat from his forehead and clicked *1 mile*. All the markers disappeared, except one. One blue marker that identified the neighborhood where John's family lived. Adrenaline flooded into his bloodstream.

He hovered the curser over the marker and clicked. A small photo of his face popped up along with his name: Quisenberry, John. In addition to his height, weight, and birthday, the site displayed their home address. Hot tears burned his eyes. Below his birthdate, John clicked the words: *More Info*. The photo, taken during his annual registration at the police department, enlarged to fill half the screen. "*Jesus Christ*! A description loomed in bold letters: *Lewd or Lascivious Acts with a Child under 14.*

John stared at the image. He'd never bothered to look, never wanted to see the photos taken at the station. Each year, filled with humiliation, he faced the camera. The clerk behind the lens regarded him as filth. His crime screamed he belonged to the lowest scum of the earth. The picture on the computer screen aged him, his face gray in pallor. If he had an older brother, this could be him. The contrast of his photo displayed in the company brochure struck him. There he stood proud, a big smile radiating the confidence of a man who appeared to be on top of the world. The face staring back at him showed a worthless human being, eyes filled with despair.

John shut down the computer and hurried to the bathroom. Yanking paper towels from the dispenser, he ran them under cold water and pressed them to his face. His own reflection made him want to punch the mirror, break it into pieces. *Just kill yourself.* He buried his face in his hands and slid to the floor. *They're better off without me.*

Chapter 26

Diana walked through the front door just as Melissa grabbed her jacket from the coat rack. "You're home early. What about practice?"

Her daughter walked right by, mumbling, "I don't feel good."

"Are you sick?"

The bedroom door slammed.

"I'll be right back," Melissa called upstairs. "I'm walking over to get Lucy from school." She turned the doorknob. Homer came running and danced around her feet. "Yes, you can come, Mister." Melissa held tight to the leash as the dog pulled her through the front door. The fresh October air invigorated her. It had been a while since she had a decent night's sleep. Some of the neighbors had Halloween decorations in their yards. Across the street, Kate pulled weeds around alona huge blowup pumpkin.

"Your yard looks great!" Melissa called.

Kate stood and brushed the dirt from her hands. Her curly brown hair was tied up in a blue checkered bandana. "I'm working on it!"

Melissa continued walking. She tried to gauge whether Kate's friendliness was genuine or forced. Did she know about John?

The kindergarteners were lined up by the gate waiting for a

parent or sibling to pick them up. Within a few months, these same children would venture home alone if they lived close by. Melissa still remembered in vivid detail the first time Kevin—and two years later Diana—asked if they could walk home on their own. She started by meeting them halfway. By the end of the year, she watched from the window, knowing the exact moment her children would come into view.

Lucy ran to her. "Hi, Mommy!"

Melissa knelt and wrapped her in a hug. "How was your first day?"

The teacher approached. "She did great!" "I have a feeling this transition will be very easy for her. Lucy already knows a couple of kids from the neighborhood. By the end of the week, I'm willing to bet she'll be friends with everybody."

Relief washed over Melissa. "Such good news! Thank you." She handed the dog's leash to her daughter, and Lucy skipped along the sidewalk playing hopscotch. "Mama, Kate's outside. Can we go look at her decorations?"

She was anxious to get home to Diana but took Lucy's hand and crossed the street.

"Hi, Kate," Lucy called. "Your yard looks so pretty! I love all the big pumpkins and skeletons."

"Why, thank you," Kate said. "I always have so much fun decorating. Our kids don't seem to enjoy them like they used to."

"How are they doing?" Melissa asked. Although they lived across the street, their children stopped spending time together when they entered middle school.

"Jeffrey won first place in the science competition," Kate said, "and Lindsay spends most of the time in her room practicing the clarinet. They don't have much time to converse with us these days."

Melissa detected a hint of dismay.

"I suppose it could be worse though," Kate continued. "At least they aren't getting into trouble."

"Our kids aren't much different," Melissa said. "Football, cheerleading, all things more exciting than hanging out with parents." She patted Lucy on the head. "We're fortunate to have this one here who still enjoys spending time with Mom and Dad."

Kate looked up as if remembering something. "Hey, we're having a small gathering the night before Halloween if your family wants to stop by. Just some friends from Craig's department, Ann and Connor from up the street, and their friends, the Medfords. We thought it would be fun to dress up. We'll have appetizers and drinks—early since it's a school night. We'd love to see your family. It's been a long time."

"Can we go, Mommy?" Lucy tugged on her sleeve. "Pretty please?"

John couldn't stand Craig, Kate's husband. He wasn't Melissa's favorite either—chauvinist that he was. But other neighbors would be there, so it might be okay. Surely Kate wouldn't invite them if she knew. "Let me talk to John, but I'm sure it will be fine. Can I bring anything?"

"Nope. It's all taken care of."

"Okay, we'll see you next week."

"Bye, Kate!" Lucy waved.

Back home, Melissa sliced an apple with a scoop of peanut butter for Lucy and inserted *The Little Mermaid* into the VCR. The movie had remained in their television cabinet since Kevin and Diana were little. It was one of those movies where the whole family knew the words to every song. She headed upstairs and knocked on Diana's door before peeking in. Curled on her bed, Diana stared out the window. "Hey, are you okay?" Melissa put the back of her hand on Diana's forehead."

"It's not that, Mom, I'm fine. I mean I'm not sick or anything."

"Are you getting your period?"

Diana shook her head.

"Do you want to talk about it?" She hoped to God this wasn't about a boy. Diana was only thirteen. Some of her friends were already talking about "going out" with boys from the football team.

Her back to Melissa, Diana's voice wavered. "Today in study hall we got to look up stuff on the computer. Johnny said all the sex offenders in town were listed on a website. Everyone crowded around him. I was afraid they were going to see Daddy." She turned to her mom, tears filling her big green eyes. "Is that the site he's on, Mom?"

Melissa froze. "Oh, Honey, I'm so sorry."

"After you guys talked to me and Kevin, I told Marie about the website. Please don't be mad. She's my best friend. Anyway, when Johnny said that in class, Marie could tell I was going to cry, so she asked him if he was a weirdo who liked to look at perverts. Some of the kids started teasing him and he got mad and said, 'I'm not a pervert. I don't care who's on the list.'" Diana's voice broke. "I was so scared, Mommy."

Melissa shook inside. "Oh, Honey." She stroked her daughter's arm.

"I almost threw up, so I came home. What does it say he did, Mom? I mean, what's so bad that he's been put on a website?"

Melissa saw the confusion in her daughter's eyes. She knew it would only be a matter of time before her children asked more questions. Still, she felt completely unprepared to venture into this territory. "Daddy and a bunch of friends went camping. He had too much to drink. Do you remember he said he stopped drinking in his twenties? Well, this is the reason why. He tried to comfort a little girl who was crying. Because he had been drinking, he fell asleep next to her. Her parents were afraid he may have hurt her, so they called the police."

"If he didn't do anything, why did they put him on the internet?"

"He took what they call a plea bargain, agreeing to take part of the blame. It protected him from going to jail. If he had known this could happen all these years later, he would have made a different decision. Grandma and Grandpa were afraid too. He was so young."

"Grandma and Grandpa know?" Diana looked horrified.

"Yes, but I doubt they know about the website. They don't have a computer and aren't up to date with things like the internet." She smoothed Diana's hair from her forehead. "You know Daddy. He'd never hurt a fly."

Her daughter stared out the window as if a million miles away. Who could blame her? Melissa looked around her room at the telltale signs of transition from little girl to teenager. Diana still had stuffed animals, but instead of displaying them on the shelves of her bookcase, they now hung in a fishing net from the ceiling. She'd read about the idea in *Seventeen* magazine, so one Saturday Diana asked John to take her to the hardware store. They came back with a bright green net and hung it from the ceiling. The animals, suspended in the air, looked over the room as if guarding Diana while she slept. Her bulletin board, once filled with colorful artwork and cartoon characters, now displayed photos of friends and ticket stubs from movies.

"What happens if the kids at school find out? My friends love Daddy because he's the only dad who jokes with them." Diana fought back tears. "What if they don't want me on the cheerleading team anymore?"

"Oh, my sweet girl, they won't blame you for this." Melissa's mind raced. *Where's the website for murderers and kidnappers*? She wanted to scream.

The sound of the front door startled them. "Anybody home?" John called.

A shadow passed over Diana's face. "Please don't tell Daddy! I don't want him to know."

Melissa's gut twisted at her daughter's despair. She kissed Diana's forehead and nodded. She closed the door and headed down the stairs.

Lucy held John captive, excited to recount her first day of school. He'd been driving aimlessly until five o'clock attempting to pull himself together before arriving home. After his conversation with Gail, and the horror of viewing the website, he couldn't bear to be in the office.

Lucy continued, "And then Camille asked if I wanted to sit next to her during story time, and I said, 'of course' and Miss Stillman read us a book about Silo and Roy who are penguins that fall in love. They had a baby penguin. Camille is five like me, and she has freckles, too!"

Melissa walked in, looking as if she carried the weight of the world on her shoulders. Unless he had to, John would keep the uncertainty of his job to himself. He ruffled Lucy's hair. "I'm so happy for you! I can't wait to hear more, but first I'm going to ask Mommy about her day. He followed Melissa into the kitchen and pulled her into a hug. "Your hair smells like cigarettes."

She turned from him and opened the oven. "Oh, one of the parents was smoking when I picked Lucy up."

He frowned. "They shouldn't allow smoking near the school."

"Yeah, who knows?" she said. "We visited with Kate on our walk home. She invited us to a Halloween celebration at their house next Thursday. It's early in the evening so I told her I'd check with you, but I'd like to go.

"I suppose her husband will be there?" John said, half-kidding.

Melissa shot him a look. "Other neighbors, too."

He wondered if a gathering would ease her mind. Maybe it was the kind of thing she needed. How had he taken it for granted? Days that ran from one to the other, homework, football practice, Friday night pizza. He'd never given a thought to the loveliness of an uneventful life.

"Is everything alright?" she asked. "You seem a million miles away."

"Oh, I've got a tough client keeping me on my toes. I'm exhausted." He changed the subject. "Lucy had a good day?"

Melissa lit up. "I really enjoyed walking her to school. It reminded me of those sweet days with Kevin and Di."

"The kids are at practice?"

"Kevin should be home any minute." Melissa took some tomatoes from the refrigerator and placed them on the cutting board. "Diana left school early because she didn't feel well."

"Is she okay?" John said.

"Just an upset stomach. She's lying down in her room."

"Well then, if you don't need me, I'll jump in the shower." He turned her toward him. "I love you, Mel. I hope you know how much." The unspoken sorrow in her eyes felt like a punch to his gut. He released her and headed upstairs.

Kevin burst into the kitchen, Cole following close behind.

"Hi, Mrs. Q!" Cole's voice boomed. "Man, it smells good in here!"

"Cole, you can smell dinner a mile away," Melissa teased.

"You know me, Mrs. Q, I'm a sucker for a good meal!"

She laughed. Her son had a handful of friends, but Cole was her favorite; the only one who took time to interact with her. Kevin grabbed a full container of orange juice from the refrigerator and carried it out of the room. "We're gonna play Nintendo till dinner," he called.

Melissa turned to Cole. "I assume this means you're staying?"

His dark eyes sparkled. "That would be great!"

Chapter 27

John tried to muster up courage before entering the building. One week passed since his conversation with Gail. Like a ticking timebomb, he waited for a response from her. Each day he feared would be his last. *No news is good news*, he reminded himself. Squared shoulders, he entered the building. As usual, Bonnie didn't look up from her phone when he passed by. Her rudeness steamed him, but he greeted her with a cheery, "Good morning! Hope you have a good day."

He jumped when his phone buzzed later that morning. The red light indicated it was Gail. Shaken, John picked up the receiver. He tried to sound nonchalant. "Hi, good morning."

"Do you have a few minutes to chat?"

"Uh, sure." Beads of sweat broke out on his forehead. "I'll be right in." John looked around the office. After this meeting, he may have to pack his belongings. He tucked in his shirt, smoothed his slacks, and stepped into the hall.

"Come in. Sit." Gail gestured to the couch.

"Thanks, but I prefer to stand." His body was jacked up like a live wire.

"I know this hasn't been easy," Gail spoke with compassion, "but I wanted to be sure I had all the facts before we spoke. I conferred at length with Steven Mitchell, the Regional Manager. I brought this dilemma to his attention and asked him to research the legalities of employing someone with your background. I assured him you are, and have always been, one of our top employees. I let him know that personally, I would hate to see this past conviction jeopardize your career. I'm on your side, John."

Emotion caught in his throat. "Thank you." He respected Gail. The fact she supported him meant a great deal. "I appreciate your confidence in me."

"John, really. Sit down." She let out a small laugh. "Your pacing makes me nervous."

He wiped the sweat from his forehead, loosened his tie, and sat.

"Steven and I met last night." Gail reached for a sheet of paper with scribbled writing. It seems the law is in your favor." She smirked as if pleased. "According to Section 290.46 in the California Penal Code, the law protects offenders from additional punishment or retribution once they've paid their debt to society." Gail put down her notes. "Unless the workplace contains obvious persons at risk, such as an environment with direct access to children, an employer is required by law to treat any employee listed on Megan's Law as they would any other worker."

John heard the breath escape his lungs. How long had he been holding it? "So, wait," he stammered, "this means I can stay?"

"It does," she said. "I'm very happy with this decision. I recognize that working here may still be challenging for you, but trust that things will return to normal in time. You're a good man, John, and a fine employee."

He wanted to cry. It meant so much to know someone believed in him. He reached across the desk and shook her hand. "Thank you, Gail. You have no idea what this means to me."

Melissa met him at the front door with a frown. "A letter from the Department of Justice came for you."

Still upbeat from his conversation with Gail, John had walked up the driveway with a skip in his step. Now, meeting her gaze, his mood shifted. She handed him the envelope. "Here."

Every day Melissa had grown more anxious and withdrawn. Today, dark circles ringed her eyes. Aching to feel her body next to his he pulled her into an embrace, wishing to close the gap that grew day by day. "First, I want to give my wife a hug."

She pushed him away. "I didn't open it, but I want to know what it says."

John released her, grabbed the letter, and headed to the kitchen for some water. She followed close behind, hovering, while he filled the glass and took a drink. He slid the paper from the envelope.

Pursuant to Proposition 69: DNA Fingerprint, Unsolved Crime and Innocence Protection Act regarding the collection and use of criminal offender DNA samples, is to be modified and expanded. Therefore, any felony offense specified in Section 290 is required to provide the following: buccal swab samples, right thumbprint, and a full palm print impression of each hand, and any blood specimens or other biological samples required for identification analysis. If you have received this notification, you must contact your local law enforcement agency within ten days to schedule an appointment.

"What does it say?" She grabbed the letter and began to read.

John recalled the news article from 1987, four years after his own conviction. Tommie Lee Andrews became the first person in the United States to be convicted of rape based on DNA evidence.

Melissa shoved the letter at him. "What does this mean?"

"I have to go to the police station to provide DNA samples."

"But why? It's been years since your court stuff."

"Looks like every person convicted of a sex crime is now required to have their DNA on file."

"But I don't want your DNA on file!" she shrieked.

He put his hand on her shoulder, trying to calm her. "This is a good thing, Mel. If a crime is committed, running a sample of DNA found at the scene would eliminate me from being a suspect."

"It's not just this stupid DNA thing!" she yelled. "Your name is blasted all over the internet. Now this. It never stops! Our kids worry every day someone at school will see you on the sex offender site. This DNA crap is just one more thing, one more reminder that our lives will never be normal again."

John reached for her, but she pushed him away. He dropped his arms and stepped back. She'd never lashed out like this. "What do you want me to do, Melissa? Move out of the house? Would you rather I not live here?" His voice rose. "I can do that—move to an apartment on the other side of the tracks. Is that what you want? To pretend you aren't married to me!" Spittle sprayed from his mouth. "The kids will still have my name, Melissa! I'll still be their father!"

Her shoulders slumped. "I just thought maybe we could move to a place where nobody knows us."

"And what? Give up my job? Make the kids change schools?"

"I'm just throwing ideas around," she whimpered. "Every time I go to the store or gym, I see people we know, and wonder if they know. I can't even have a conversation without imagining what they think, Poor Melissa! Did she know he was a child molester before she married him? Who would allow someone like that around her children?" Mel heaved with emotion. "They might even think I don't know about it. Like I'm an idiot!"

"Wow." His voice was tight. "I guess I didn't know you were so worried about what other people think."

"Oh, come on, John!" Exasperation poured from her, "I wish I could be that person who doesn't have a care in the world, but I'm not. Maybe I could do a better job if I didn't have three innocent children who are forced to live with this. You don't even know how much it's affecting them. Diana came home panicked the other day because the kids in her class looked up Megan's Law on the computer!"

"Oh, God. Is she okay?" The revelation took the wind out of his sails. John couldn't stomach his daughter being tormented because of his actions. He slumped into the chair. "What do you want me to do?" he whispered, begging for direction. "Would you like to divorce me, so your name isn't associated with mine? I can get my own place, Mel, with an address not linked to our house. It would probably be better for you and the kids."

Melissa rested a hand on his arm. "I'm sorry. I'm on edge from not sleeping. And those rare times I do fall asleep; I have nightmares of people coming to the house demanding to take our children." She broke into sobs. "I don't know what to do. I'm a total mess."

He decided to put it all on the table. "Everyone at work knows."

Mel's face went white. "What?"

"Yep, a couple of coworkers found my name on the website. They went to Gail."

"Oh no! What's going to happen?"

"The good news is, she investigated the legalities, and for once, the law is on my side. I can't be terminated for my record, but…" his voice trailed off. "I've gone to work every day thinking I might get fired. Not to mention putting up with stares and water cooler gossip from people I considered friends. It's been hell."

"Why didn't you tell me?"

"Tell you? Really? Like I'm going to add more stress to your life?"

A look of sorrow clouded her face. "I'm so sorry. I've been consumed by what other people are thinking and so worried for the kids, I didn't stop to think about your job, or how you were handling everything."

"All I've ever wanted," John said, "is to make you happy. To provide a good life for you and the kids. I don't want to lose you, Mel. I'd have nothing to live for. Tears rolled down his face. "I just don't know how to fix what's happened."

She pulled him close. "We'll figure it out."

They held each other until Melissa whispered, "I have to get Lucy from Camille's. Kevin and Diana should be home in the next hour."

"Don't worry about dinner. I can rummage something up. I'll have it ready when the kids get home."

Melissa kissed his forehead. "Diana didn't want me to tell you about the computer incident because she doesn't want you to worry. It would probably be better if you didn't mention it."

"I won't say a word," he said. She turned to leave, but he pulled her back. "Mel, I'm willing to do anything to protect you and the kids, even if it means moving out."

"I know you are. Let's not think about it right now."

Chapter 28

D o we have to goooooo?" Diana dragged out the sentence. "It will be fun," chirped Melissa. She knelt by Lucy with an eyebrow pencil, carefully drawing whiskers on her cheeks.

"But there's nobody I want to see," Diana whined. "It will be a big waste of my time."

"I'm sure Lindsay will be happy to see you."

"No, she won't, Mom. She's weird. I never see her at school. She hangs out with the geek crowd."

"Diana, be nice. I'm sure you can find something to talk about. You and Lindsay used to play together for hours."

"Maybe when we were little kids playing Barbies. Trust me, we have nothing to talk about. If you force me to go, I'm not dressing up like an idiot. I'll show up as I am."

"Suit yourself," Melissa said. She'd learned some arguments weren't worth having.

Kevin opened the refrigerator. "I'm going as a professional football player." He hadn't changed his uniform after practice and reapplied black eye grease. It now dripped down his face.

John stepped into the kitchen. "Nice look, Kev. Are you going as Alice Cooper?"

"Ha-ha. Funny, Dad. I'd rather be Alice Cooper than whoever

you're trying to impersonate in that orange spotted dress."

John stepped in front of Melissa. "Honey, your caveman has arrived." He pounded his chest a few times.

Diana rolled her eyes. "Dad, you're not Tarzan, you're Fred Flintstone.

Melissa stood and kissed him. "Well, don't you look handsome!"

"And look at you!" John gave her a little twirl. "Who knew Wilma could be so sexy!"

"Gross," Kevin and Diana said in unison.

Kate greeted them at the door. "Welcome, welcome!" She wore a sequined jumpsuit and long, black wig. Bangles jingled from her forearms. She must have noticed their quizzical expressions. "Cher," she offered. "You'll find Sonny at the bar."

"Oh, of course," Melissa said. "Love the jewelry!"

"And you must be the Flintstones!" Kate exclaimed, ushering them inside. She patted Lucy's head, "Well isn't this the cutest mouse I've ever seen. I seem to remember your sister in this very same costume. Kevin, Di, the teens are in the game room. There's plenty of food and drinks."

"Great," Diana muttered under her breath.

John nudged her. "Be nice."

"The younger kids are watching a video, Lucy." Kate gestured to the den. "I'm sure they would love to have a sweet mouse join them."

John and Melissa joined the guests in the great room. Craig, dressed in tight black corduroy bell bottoms, a retro wig, and droopy mustache, made an ideal Sonny Bono. A paisley polyester shirt unbuttoned to the navel showed off his well-defined chest. Years of military service kept him fit, unlike John who had grown soft around the middle. He was suddenly embarrassed by his Flintstone costume.

"Hey, looks like Fred and Wilma have arrived," Craig announced from the bar. "Would you like something to drink?" He motioned to a table displaying a giant pumpkin-shaped bowl. It appeared to have smoke pouring from it. "Kate concocted a ghoulish drink." He looked directly at John his dark eyes flat. "It's kiddie punch. No alcohol."

John squirmed at the undercurrent of Craig's tone. He did not meet his host's eyes. "Looks interesting."

Craig shifted his gaze to Melissa. "And what about you, beautiful? Can I get you something stronger?"

"Thanks, but not right now. I think I'll try the punch."

"Have it your way." He looked her up and down, then let out a slow whistle, "Man oh man, Wilma looks good on you."

John stepped forward fists clenched. "Hey!"

"Settle down, buddy boy, I'm just giving your wife a well-deserved compliment."

Melissa squeezed his arm and pulled him from the bar. "It's not worth it," she muttered under her breath.

"He's obviously drunk," John said. "Steer clear of him unless you're with me."

Craig's voice escalated as the evening wore on. "Those antiwar protestors are a bunch of liberal pansies. We gotta maintain a US presence in Iraq to develop a democracy. Some men don't have the balls to stand up for our own country."

Melissa gave John the *get me the hell outta here* look. She headed toward the den to round up the kids. He walked over to the bar where Craig mixed another drink. "We're heading out," John said. "Need to get the kids home. School tomorrow."

Craig placed an orange slice on the rim of the glass and licked his fingers. "Hey, what about that wife of yours? Are you going to hit her over the head with a club? Drag her to the bedroom like a real caveman?" He snickered. "Or is she too much woman for you?"

"Hey, buddy," John seethed, "maybe you better lay off the whiskey. I think you've had enough for one night."

"Oh, is that right?" Craig chugged his drink, then slammed the glass on the counter. "Spoken by a man who drinks from the punch bowl."

John's jaw tightened. He forced himself to turn and walk away.

"Maybe you don't even fuck your wife," Craig called after him. "Maybe you like little girls instead."

John stopped in his tracks. "What did you say?"

"You heard me," Craig sneered. "Word's out you like young pussy."

John turned lightning fast, his fist faster than his thoughts. Craig stumbled backward into a table, knocking empty glasses onto the tiled floor. Remnants of ice and glass shards slid across the surface. The room fell silent.

Melissa appeared with the kids. "My God, what happened?"

John cradled his hand. "Take the kids. Leave."

"But—"

"Just do it, Mel!"

"Daddy?" Lucy squeaked.

"It's okay, Honey. Go with Mommy."

"Dad?" Kevin interjected.

"Go! All of you. I'll see you at home."

Diana shot him a look of disbelief and shook her head.

Kate appeared from the kitchen and rushed to her husband. She looked from him to John with confusion. "What in God's name is going on?"

"I'm sorry, Kate," John said.

Craig sat up but leaned against the wall for support. The Sonny wig hung over one eye; mustache askew. He rubbed his jaw and then stared at the blood on his hand.

John poked a finger an inch from Craig's face. "Don't you ever talk about me, or my wife, again," he growled. "Ever! Do you hear me?"

"I hear you."

John grabbed the knob on the front door and stopped. He turned to face the guests. "I'm sorry to all of you. I truly am."

Chapter 29

Melissa jumped at the knock on the front door. Through the peephole, she saw Kate standing on the porch holding a bundt cake. Her mind raced. It had been four days since the dreadful party. She'd barely left the house, too mortified to face the neighbors who now knew their secret. She turned the knob with shaky hands.

As if expecting the door to remain closed, Kate, half-turned, whirled around to face her. "Melissa," she said, her voice soft like a caress, "I'm so sorry." She held out the cake, her eyes glistening.

Melissa flicked away tears.

"Oh, Honey." Kate set the cake on the porch chair. "Craig's behavior was appalling. I can't believe he would do such a thing. I can assure you my opinion of John hasn't changed. I don't know what all this Megan's Law is about, but I don't care. Not one bit. I hope you can believe me."

Not able to speak from the lump in her throat, Melissa nodded.

"Craig threatened to press charges," Kate continued, "but has backed down. Frankly, I think he's embarrassed to report it."

Melissa stepped forward and hugged her. "Thanks for coming by. I appreciate your kindness." She shut the door and sank to the floor.

Melissa slogged through each day as if walking through mud. She tried to stay upbeat in front of the kids but succumbed to exhaustion at the end of the day. Yesterday, she observed two women in her yoga class, heads bent close, speaking in hushed tones. They halted their conversation when she walked in, then turned away. Face burning, Melissa unrolled her yoga mat and stared straight ahead at the instructor. Willing herself to relax, she tried to follow the breathing exercises, but her mind raced. She flashed back to the summer months when families gathered at the pool. John loved tossing the kids around and playing Marco Polo with them. Were these women now sickened that a pervert was in the water with their children? Did they blame her for being his wife?

Melissa couldn't breathe. She knelt and rolled up her mat. Everyone stared as she walked towards the door. Once inside the safety of her car, tears flowed. How had her life taken such a horrible turn? Nothing had prepared her for what their family now faced. She turned the key, put the gearshift in reverse, and accelerated. The car jerked at the sudden movement. A horn blared. She slammed on the brakes. "Dammit!" she cursed. Melissa rested her head on the steering wheel to catch her breath, then drove straight to the nearest convenience store.

"I'll have a pack of Virginia Slims." She did not meet the cashier's eyes. Heat rushed to her face. She didn't dare look around the store, for fear she might recognize someone. *It's not like I'm buying drugs for goodness' sake.* Still, the guilt nagged her. "May I have a pack of matches also?"

The clerk reached behind him and set both on the counter. "That'll be $6.75. Would you like a receipt?"

"No, thank you."

Melissa drove to a nearby park and walked to the furthest picnic table. She lit a cigarette and inhaled deeply. The smell of sulfur and tobacco wafted over her. She stared at the clouds, puffed out her cheeks, and blew smoke rings into the air. This little rebellion excited her, as it had as a teen. John didn't touch anything stronger than the endless cups of coffee he consumed daily. He had bragged that once he got sober, he relinquished his vices. To him, any addiction was a sign of weakness. But Melissa didn't feel weak. She felt as if she was in control of at least one fucking thing in her life. She took another drag.

Chapter 30

The front door burst open. Kevin and Cole appeared in the kitchen.

"How was practice?" Melissa shouted over the clatter of cleats.

"It sucked!" Kevin barked. He threw down his helmet and with one swift kick, he sent it spinning across the room. It slammed into the sliding glass door and rolled across the floor. He stormed out of the room. "I'm taking a shower."

Melissa caught sight of his red, swollen cheek and remnants of a bloody nose. The pungent smell of sweat trailed behind him. She tried not to breathe it in. "What happened to your face?" she called, fighting the urge to follow him. The air stilled as if a tornado had just blown through, leaving her and Cole in the aftermath. "What in the world?" she exclaimed. "What happened?"

Cole stared at his muddy cleats. "Some guys on the team were being jerks. They kinda got into it."

"Got into what? A fight?" Though Kevin's size could be intimidating, gentleness exuded from him. She'd never known him to get into a physical altercation with anybody. "Tell me what's going on."

The boy shifted from one foot to the other, as if weighing his words. "A couple of the guys said some stuff about Mr. Q. Kevin flew off the handle. I've never seen him like that! He jumped on Brad Davies, the biggest guy on the team. Just pummeled him. The coach had to break them up, but Brad punched him in the face first."

Melissa pulled a chair from the table and sat. She pressed her legs to the floor to steady their shaking. The sound of gurgling potatoes filled the room. "What did they say?"

Cole sat down next to her. He picked at a loose thread on his white football pants, now dirty and stained with grass. He wouldn't meet her eyes.

"Cole?" she prodded. "You can tell me."

The boy glanced at her, then quickly down at his fidgety hands. "We walked into the locker room, and the guys were laughing about something. When they saw us, they shut up like they didn't want us to hear."

Melissa recalled her yoga class. Her stomach clenched.

"Brad started to say something, but one of the guys elbowed him. Told him to shut his mouth. I didn't know what was up, but Kevin yelled, 'Dude, if you have something to say, say it to my face.' The other guys teased Brad saying, 'Yeah Dude, if you have something to say, say it to his face.'"

She braced herself. "And?"

Cole stacked and unstacked the placemats.

"You can tell me."

This time he fixed his gaze on her. "Brad called Mr. Q a pedophile. Said he likes to fondle little girls. Kevin shoved him. He said Brad didn't know what he was talking about. Brad told him to look at the sex offender site, said his dad's mugshot was on it, and everyone had seen it. Kev lost it. I tried to pull him back, but he had so much rage he even took a swing at me! The coach broke it up."

Melissa struggled to gather her thoughts. "Is this something he's talked to you about?"

"Kevin told me his dad got arrested for something a long time ago but that it wasn't a big deal. He didn't say what for, and I didn't push him."

Melissa felt like she'd been kicked in the gut. This thing grew like wildfire, spreading to every area of their lives. Helpless to stop it, she could only stand in its wake. She wanted to cry, but not in front of Cole.

The front door opened. "Anybody home?" John called.

Cole met Melissa's eyes.

"In here," she said.

"Hey, you two, where's the rest of the gang?"

Melissa tried to keep her voice even. "Lucy's napping. Diana and Marie are still at cheerleading practice. Kevin is taking a shower."

"Dinner smells great!" He kissed her on the cheek. "Can I help with anything?" He opened the oven. The earthy smell of roasted chicken and herbs wafted through the room. "This looks fantastic! I smelled it before I walked in the door." He rested a hand on Cole's shoulder. "Are you joining us for dinner, Pal?"

"No, I'm going to head home. I have a history test tomorrow." Cole pushed his chair from the table. "Thanks for the invite. I'll join next time."

Once the front door shut behind him, Melissa covered her face and let out a sob.

"Honey, what is it?" John pulled the chair close. He removed her hands and tilted her face to his. "Look at me, Mel. What is it?"

"Kevin got into a fight today. The guys on the team harassed him about the website."

John slammed his hand on the table. "Fuck!" He stood so fast the chair banged to the floor.

Melissa jumped at the sound. "Please calm down!" she admonished in a hushed tone. "I don't want Lucy to hear you."

John pushed past her. "I need to get out of here."

The front door slammed. Melissa blinked in surprise.

"Mommy," Lucy whimpered. "Where's Daddy going?"

Their tiny daughter stood in the doorway, trembling. She clutched her favorite blanket to her face. The sound of screeching tires filled the room. Lucy's eyes went wide like saucers. Melissa picked her up and held her close, disguising the worry in her voice,

"Daddy has to go take care of some business at work."

"But I heard yelling," Lucy croaked.

Melissa nuzzled her daughter's neck. The sweet aroma of bananas and baby shampoo made her want to weep.

"Daddy got a call to return to the office. It made him angry because he wanted to stay home with us." She cringed at the lie. "Would you like to help me get dinner ready? I'll get out the salad fixings, and you can put them in the bowl. It would be a big help to me."

Lucy pulled a stool over to the counter. "I think I should be wearing my apron, Mama."

Melissa smiled and pulled Lucy's favorite from the drawer. A gift from Donna, "Sweet Little Niece" was embroidered on the front. It might be just the girls tonight, with John gone and Kevin locked in his room. Her stomach churned at the thought of food. Lucy's delicate fingers tore each lettuce leaf in half before dropping them into the teak bowl. She rested a hand on her daughter's small back. "Would you like to put the rolls on the baking sheet?"

Lucy nodded.

Melissa pulled a can of Pillsbury Pop & Fresh from the refrigerator. Lucy loved watching the can pop open, the dough oozing from the cracks. She put her hands over Lucy's. Together they called, "One, two, three!" and struck the can against the counter. Lucy giggled when it popped open. She carefully pulled apart each piece of dough and set them on the baking sheet.

Melissa lifted her from the stool. "How about we start a video until it's time to eat? You haven't watched *Lion King* in a while." Lucy climbed onto the couch. She wrapped the blanket around her wrist and put her thumb in her mouth. Melissa hadn't seen her do this in a long time. *One more thing to worry about.* She kissed Lucy's cheek. "I'll call you when dinner's ready." She debated if she should go upstairs to check on Kevin. She'd hoped John would speak to him. Maybe she could knock on his door and ask if he felt like talking; new territory for her. *Why has this fallen into my lap?* The injustice filled her with resentment.

Chapter 31

Blinded by rage, John flew out of the driveway. He pulled onto the freeway, telling himself he'd find an AA meeting. Paul left a message earlier that week reminding him of a nightly meeting at the Congregational Church. He could at least give it a try. Moments later, he passed the exit. The next off-ramp would take him to Ernie's Liquors. He slowed and put on his blinker. There wouldn't be any chance of running into someone who knew him in this seedy part of the city. Every fiber in his being told him to turn around, go home, but an invisible force propelled him forward. It had been twenty-two years since he drank. The thought of blowing it scared and excited him at the same time. "Why the fuck not?" His voice sounded loud, defiant. It was only a matter of time before Melissa took the kids and left him anyway.

John parked in the furthest spot from the store. He stepped from his car and scanned the lot. Empty. Cautiously he opened the front door, startled by the high-pitched bell. His eyes darted back and forth, taking in the colorful bottles. He hadn't been inside a liquor store in years. Blood pumped through his veins. It felt as scandalous as being in a whore house.

John put the bottle on the counter.

The clerk reached for it. "How ya doin' tonight?"

"Not so good," John said.

The man nodded, took the bills, and put a fifth of vodka in a small brown paper bag. "Well, good luck to you."

"Thank you. Have a good night."

John's head darted back and forth searching the dark parking lot. The lonesome sound of a train whistle pierced him. An urge to chuck the bottle appealed to his wiser self, but it lasted only a moment. John locked the car doors, tilted the seat back, and stretched his legs. He grabbed his box of CDs which he rarely listened to anymore. He hunted for "Don't Look Back" his favorite Boston album from high school. John skipped to the track he listened to on repeat after Jenny dumped him. *It's getting harder every day for me, to hide behind this dream you see, a man I'll never be.* Same lyrics, different woman.

He turned up the volume and removed the bottle from the bag. He unscrewed the lid and took a deep inhale. The familiar smell of ethanol shot right into his brain. His eyes watered. Raising the bottle to his lips, he took a long swig. The alcohol went down easier than expected. A familiar heat bloomed in his chest, an exhilarating rush to his bloodstream. How he had missed it! This moment of bliss, as if being reunited with a past lover; the taste, the smell, the excitement of something not quite forgotten, a sensation that had been there always, lurking beneath the surface, waiting to be brought to life. John luxuriated in the numbing, almost erotic effect as it spread across his body.

The cold car roused John from his stupor. He was shocked to see four hours had passed. Melissa would be so worried. He rubbed his hands together until the warmth returned. Inside the glovebox he found an old container of Altoids mints. He popped two in his mouth. Eyes wide, he blinked a few times to clear his vision before putting the car in reverse. He stopped at the first gas station, tossed the bottle into the overflowing trash bin, and splashed cold water on his face. John looked at himself in the mirror with disgust. He couldn't let this happen again.

When he pulled into the driveway, Melissa stood on the porch, eyes crazed. "Where have you been?" she yelled. How long had she waited for him? He walked toward her, one step in front of the other. She tightened her robe and trembled. "Where were you?" she demanded. "I've been worried sick!"

Careful to enunciate each word, John spoke. "I…went…to…a…meeting. Needed to clear my head."

"This long?"

"I had coffee with some of the guys."

"Your eyes are bloodshot," she said. It sounded like an accusation.

"I've been crying, Melissa. This whole thing makes me want to give up. I thought going to a meeting would help." The lies came easily. He pulled her into his arms, hoping the mints disguised the alcohol. "I'm sorry I worried you. You deserve better than this, better than me."

She rubbed his back. "Just come inside." Her voice was softer now. "We'll talk about this in the morning." Taking his hand, she led him through the door.

Inside the safety of his home, John collapsed against the wall. "I don't know what I'd do without you, Mel." He slid to the floor. "I'm so afraid of losing you. Sometimes I wish I had a gun so I could shoot myself."

Melissa stared in disbelief. He was blabbering, wiping tears and snot from his nose with the sleeve of his jacket. His wife had never seen him so undone. She knelt beside him and tried to pull his limp body into her arms. "It's late. Let's get you into the shower."

John allowed her to help him stand. He followed her to the bedroom, promising himself he would put this night behind him. She deserved better.

Chapter 32

Something was off with John. Melissa couldn't pinpoint exactly what it was, but ever since returning late that night after Kevin's fight, he appeared preoccupied. Her husband spoke to her as if a million miles away. Even his playful banter with the kids sounded forced. She dialed Donna's number. "Hi, it's me."

"Oh, hi! How's everyone doing?"

Her sister's voice immediately soothed her nerves. Melissa leaned against the wall and wrapped the telephone cord around her hand. "I'm okay. Well, not really. I think either I'm going crazy, or John is. Maybe it's both of us." She heard the rumble of the dishwasher in the background. Donna was probably tidying up the kitchen after her husband Clive left for work.

"What's going on?" her sister asked. "I mean, aside from the obvious."

"Something is off with John. I can't really explain it, but it's like he's checked out."

"Well, gosh, the man must be going through hell, Melissa. I can't imagine how he gets up every morning and goes to work."

Melissa sighed. "I get that it's challenging, but this is different. It's almost like he's had a mental break, like he's dissociated from reality, from the family. He avoids eye contact with me. It's like he's looking through me, not at me."

"Have you talked to him about it?"

"I ask him every day if something is going on, but he gets sarcastic and says, 'I guess what I'm going through isn't enough.' For a while, he acted surly, pissed off. That I understood. This is something else entirely. It's like I'm living with a stranger."

"Maybe you two should see a counselor," Donna suggested. "Someone to help you navigate this nightmare. I mean, honestly, it may be too much to handle on your own."

"I'm not sure John would be open to it, but I'll give it some thought."

"Please keep me posted, Sis. I love you."

"Me, too," Melissa's voice cracked. "You're still planning to come for Thanksgiving, right? John's parents are dying to see you."

"Definitely. Alex will be home from college earlier in the week. The three of us will come bearing pies and homemade apple cider."

Melissa sat for a moment after they hung up. She didn't want to step back into her life.

John balked when his wife suggested the two of them talk to a professional. Melissa insisted an unbiased third party might help with their "family issues". John couldn't think of anything worse than discussing their private lives with a stranger. On the other hand, Mel asked for so little, he acquiesced. Now they sat in a refurbished Victorian in downtown San Mateo.

Molly Greene was a Marriage & Family therapist who specialized in working with couples. Her pale blue office shimmered with soft lighting giving the impression of candlelight. Photographs hung on the walls displaying flowers in various stages of bloom. Colorful pillows decorated the beige couch. Her bookshelf, packed to overflowing, contained titles such as *The Seven Principles for Making Marriage Work* and *Getting Unstuck*.

After sharing a detailed introduction as to who they were and the makeup of their family, Molly asked what brought them to see her. Melissa jumped right in, explaining how the publication of

John's name on Megan's Law had affected their family. Her eyes filled with tears when she recounted the neighborhood Halloween party, Lucy's change of schools, Diana's panic in the computer lab, and Kevin's recent fight. Tears rolled down her cheeks as she launched into her worry about running into someone who knew about the site, and her fear of confiding in her closest friend Vicky, who would probably hate her for not being truthful about John's past. She topped it off by declaring she felt like a prisoner trapped in her own home.

John stared dumbstruck. The immensity of her pain hit him like a brick.

Molly turned to him. "How do you feel about what Melissa shared?"

Streaks of gray ran through Molly's dark hair. He guessed her to be ten to fifteen years older than them. She had kind eyes. They searched his now, awaiting a response. He stared at the floor. He didn't have the words his wife used so freely. "I feel terrible, of course I do. If I could do anything to fix it, I would, but I just don't know how."

"I know he feels horrible," Melissa said, "which makes me feel even worse. I want to get through this, but every day we drift further apart."

Before she could continue, Molly held up her hand. "Would you please look at John and tell him how you feel?"

Melissa hesitated. Fidgeting, she turned to him. "Honey, you're acting different. I mean, of course, this whole thing is taxing, but instead of drawing closer to me, you seem to be pulling away. You play and joke with the kids, but not really. It doesn't seem genuine. It's more like you're playacting at being a fun dad." Her voice trailed off. "It's like the man I know has disappeared."

"John, would you like to respond to Melissa?"

"I had to talk to my son…" John said. Tears welled up making it hard to continue.

"Please look at Melissa," Molly said, "and tell her what you're feeling."

He struggled to meet her eyes. Her deeply etched sorrow reminded him every day of how he had failed her, failed his family. "You want to know what it was like talking to our son about the fight he got into? It was humiliating, Melissa, knocking on his bedroom door like a dog with his tail between his legs. I had to explain to our firstborn child, the son I would give my life for, that there are people who believe his dad isn't just a criminal, but a pervert, a sex offender. Try to spin that to a fifteen-year-old whose popularity at school is number one."

"John, Kevin knows—"

"Stop. Let me finish. I couldn't even get mad at him for punching the guy, nor could I tell him there's a better way to handle things when I did the very same thing to Craig! I'm supposed to be the person he admires, not the crux of his embarrassment." His words found a rhythm and he didn't hold back. "I've ruined your picture-perfect life, Melissa." His anger filled the room. "I know you resent it, maybe even hate me for it."

"I don't hate you!" Melissa cried. "I hate what you're going through, what we're all going through. I feel sorry for all of us." Her voice choked with emotion, "But I still love you."

John couldn't look at her. He fixed his stare on a purple orchid in a mirrored frame. "Be honest, Mel. There's a part of you that wishes you could take the kids and walk away from this marriage, away from me. Then you wouldn't have to face this bullshit. I mean, I would if I were you. I've said it before, if things are so hard, I can leave. I'll rent an apartment and see the kids on weekends like other divorced fathers."

"If I didn't want to work through this," her voice rose, "I wouldn't have suggested we come to therapy."

"And what's therapy going to do, Melissa? How is talking about our problems going to change the fact that you're too scared to attend a fucking yoga class?"

Melissa slumped back onto the couch as if she'd given up.

Dr. Greene put aside her pad of paper. "We're coming to the end of our session. I want to say how glad I am you both came in."

Compassion sounded in her voice. "I can see you have a deep love for each other and your children. This unfortunate turn of events has deeply affected your lives." She turned to John. "You made the best decision you could at the time and are not to blame for this recent misfortune. You've created a wonderful life, with a family who love you. This is the testament to who you truly are."

John's throat constricted at her kind words.

Molly continued, "Melissa said something very important, and I want to make sure you heard it. John, would you be willing to reflect on what she said?"

Surprised to be called on, his mind raced, wondering what part of her spiel he was supposed to recall. "Uh, she feels isolated and trapped. She's embarrassed by what people think. I don't know what else."

"Did you hear her say she loves you and wants to work through this?"

"Not really."

"Melissa, would you be willing to say it again?"

Mel squirmed in her chair, then turned to him. "I don't want to live my life without you." Her voice cracked, "I just want us to be okay."

Unable to hold her gaze, his eyes dropped to his lap.

"I know this isn't easy," Molly said, "but it's essential you two keep this dialogue going. We made good progress today. I want to stress the importance of returning next week to continue our work."

They stood and grabbed their jackets from the coat rack.

John had come to the appointment directly from work, so he walked with Melissa to her car. Although only four-thirty, the dark November sky loomed over them, ominous. He opened the car door for her. Before getting in, she turned to him. "Thank you for coming with me, for giving this a shot. I'll see you at home?"

He sensed her unease, probably wondering if she had revealed too much. She now looked to him for reassurance. "I think I'll go to a meeting first. Do you mind?"

"No, of course not. We'll wait until you get home to have dinner."

"You don't have to wait. I'll probably get something to eat with the guys afterward."

"Oh, okay." She sounded hurt. "What time do you think you'll be home then?"

"Not late." John opened the car door. He looked at the sky. "It's going to rain any minute. Get in the car." He kissed her cheek and closed the door behind her.

John got in his car and drove to Menlo Park, an outlying city twenty minutes from San Mateo. Though not far in distance, it felt worlds away from the house that now confined him. True to his word, he hadn't had a drink since the night he returned home in a drunken stupor. John didn't know if it pained or relieved him that Mel bought his story. Thoughts of his binge consumed him. He now wondered if it would be possible to have a drink or two without losing control. The last two weeks proved he didn't need alcohol, but it would sure be nice to have a drink on occasion. God knows he needed one after their therapy session. If he managed to keep it in check, he didn't see how it could be a problem. The AA term, *stinkin' thinkin'* came to mind. He brushed it aside.

The rain poured when he parked in a neighborhood known as the Iron Triangle. He dashed across the street, shielding his head with his hands. The neon sign on the dive bar flashed "Rusty Nail". John could be anonymous in a place like this—unlike AA anonymity where a sense of recognition greeted him every time he walked into a meeting. Those in recovery shared a familiar struggle that used to comfort him. He didn't want to meet anyone's eyes with the implied understanding, *hey buddy, I've been there.*

John slid onto the bar stool. "Vodka on the rocks."

"You got it," the bartender said, reaching for a glass.

"With a twist of lime, please."

John ran his hand over the countertop. The slick glossy surface conjured memories of the many bars he frequented in his past life. He surveyed the dark, smoky room. Two burly guys in flannel shirts played pool. Three men sat by themselves at the bar, who, like John, probably weren't seeking conversation. The bartender put a small white napkin in front of him and set down the drink. John squeezed the lime wedge into his glass. He swirled the liquid. The sound of clinking ice cubes excited him, like a prelude to a good time. He brought the glass to his nose and inhaled. Salivating at the zesty smell of lime, mingled with vodka, John marveled that he had lived without this simple pleasure for over twenty years. He gulped it down and pushed the empty glass toward the bartender. "I'll have another." Promising to limit himself to two, he would savor the next.

The song, "Melissa" by the Allman Brothers, rang out from the jukebox. John felt a pang in his chest. He'd liked the song in high school, but it took on special meaning after he met Mel. He swallowed to soothe the rising lump in his throat. When he thought back to her standing on the porch, the frantic look on her face, he loathed himself. Never had he seen his wife look so fragile, so vulnerable. She trusted him—believed in him—even as he flat-out lied to her. Honest communication had been the foundation of their marriage. He had fractured it.

John thought of the Jenga game his family played. Each player takes a turn removing a piece of wood from the middle of the block structure, carefully replacing it on top of the tower. As blocks are pulled, the base becomes more unstable. Life is the same way. Every decision is independent of another, yet all are connected. He knew the choices he made not only affected him but his whole family. One wrong move and the tower would tumble, every decision, even the good, disappearing into a single, devastating collapse. John shook his head at the image. He'd just have to control his drinking. After the hell he'd been through, he deserved to take the edge off.

Chapter 33

S o, how has it been this past week?" Molly asked.

John stared at the therapist's hoop earrings that almost reached her chin. She wore a turquoise spiral necklace, resting on colorful scarves.

Melissa didn't waste any time. "It's been really hard. We haven't communicated about anything. I try to talk to him—" Molly's hand went up. She gestured toward John.

Melissa turned to him. "You don't talk to me anymore," she whined. "I mean aside from 'How was your day?' and 'What's for dinner?' you're distant, like you've built a shell around yourself. You don't let me in."

"I've done no such thing," he said, but Mel barely took a breath.

"We're like roommates living separate lives. We haven't made love in weeks."

"Huh!" he snorted. "It's really hard to be intimate when all I see is disdain in your eyes."

"It's not disdain," she shrieked. "I'm confused!"

"What are you confused about, Melissa? Our life has turned to shit, and it's all my fault. What more do you want me to say?"

She turned to Molly. "See, this is what I mean. He doesn't tell me how he feels, not really. He turns it back on me. Brushes it off, shuts me down."

John closed his eyes trying to tune out the nagging buzz in his ears.

"John?" Molly said. "Are you committed to this marriage?"

He blinked his eyes open. "Uh, yes."

"Melissa?"

"I am, but I need—"

Molly held up her hand. *She'd make a good referee.* John almost laughed.

"Melissa? Are you willing to do whatever it takes to stay married, even if it means not all conflicts will be resolved?"

Mel's shoulders slumped. "Yes."

Resigned to live a life of misery. He heard it in her voice.

"Some couples arrive in counseling with divorce as an option," Molly said, "so it's good to clarify we're all on the same page; that you're both willing to do what it takes to make your marriage work."

John nodded. He let his mind wander through the rest of the session. He sat up straight when Molly brought their time to a close. "Thank you for your honesty and hard work," she said. "I know it isn't easy to explore these tough emotions, and your circumstances are exceptionally challenging. Be gentle with one another. I'll see you next week."

They exited the building without saying a word.

Chapter 34

Hey, Sis, could you chop the onions for me? I need more for the stuffing."

Melissa washed her hands and pulled out the cutting board. "Yeah, yeah. Why do I always get stuck with that job?"

Donna giggled. "Because you know I can't have mascara running down my face."

Melissa's sister was a classic beauty, turning heads when she walked into a room. Under her apron, she wore a turquoise silk blouse, tucked into True Religion black jeans that fit her like a glove. She, on the other hand, wore leggings and an oversized sweater.

Thanksgiving had always been Melissa's favorite holiday. Their mother, not capable of pulling it together most years, left it to her and Donna. The two had many hilarious stories of mishaps in the kitchen, trying each year to perfect their favorite dishes. Since moving to Pasadena for Clive's job, Donna's family made the six-hour drive every year to keep up the tradition. This year Melissa had counted down the days until her sister arrived. "Thank you for being here," she said.

Donna put a hand on her shoulder, "I would never miss Thanksgiving with you. I only wish we could see each other more often. That's the hardest part about living in a new city."

Helen popped into the kitchen and surveyed the countertops. "Anything I can help with, ladies? I'm sorry I didn't check in sooner, but I've been out back with the girls. Lucy prepared a wonderful feast for me in her little kitchen, and Diana showed me all her cheerleading routines. My, that girl can move!"

John's mom was a sturdy woman with newly permed hair. She wore a dressy jogging outfit and sensible shoes. "I think we're good," Melissa said. "I know it looks like a freight train ran through the kitchen, but we'll pull it all together."

"Well, okay, if you say so,' Helen said. "I guess I'll check on the menfolk." At that moment, the living room erupted with hoots and hollers as the guys cheered for their favorite football team. The sisters glanced at each other with a look that said, *they're at it again.* "My, so much testosterone!" Helen exclaimed.

As if on cue, Donna's husband Clive called out, "Hey, Honey, can we get some more chips and dip in here?"

Donna rolled her eyes.

"Oh, let me do that." Helen grabbed a bag of potato chips and onion dip. "Helps me to feel useful. Coming right up!" she called like a short-order cook.

"I love that woman," Donna said. "And Henry, too."

Melissa nodded. "Me, too."

"We got lucky," Donna said.

Melissa heard the melancholy in her sister's voice. She suspected Donna was reminiscing about how wonderful John's parents had been when the girls lost their dad. Their mom, unable to care for herself, had to be placed in assisted living. Melissa and Donna helped get her settled, while Henry and Helen spent long hours cleaning out the house. They showed up in a way neither experienced growing up. Melissa didn't mourn Carol's death six months later but carried the pain of never having had a close relationship with her.

"John, will you please slice the turkey?" Melissa poked her head into the family room. "Donna and I will get everything on the table. Your mom is rounding up the kids."

John kissed her cheek when he passed, concentrating on each step. He had slipped into the garage and spiked his soda during the game. Nobody noticed his absences with all the hoopla going on. He didn't think he drank that much, but when he stood, a dizzying rush came over him. Retrieving the carving knife from the drawer, John turned it on. The electrical whir provided an immediate sense of satisfaction. He chuckled. *The man's job.* His wife assigned him this one task each holiday, and he prided himself on doing it well.

The sisters rushed around the kitchen pulling things from the oven, adding serving spoons to bowls, and setting dishes on the table. The bustle distracted him. *I can do this.* He carried the platter of sliced turkey into the dining room. *One step after the other.* The dog ran past him in an excited rush. John tripped. He felt the platter slip from his hands. As if in slow motion, he dove to catch it, banging his face on the corner of the table. The serving dish hit the hardwood floor with a loud clatter. Turkey flew everywhere.

Melissa appeared from the kitchen, "Oh my God! Are you okay?" She knelt in front of him. "What happened?"

John tried to focus amidst the spinning room. "I'm fine."

Homer ate turkey off the floor. Lucy picked up a leg here, a thigh there, putting the pieces back on the platter. Melissa pressed a decorative napkin to his mouth. "Let me see." She tilted his head to the light. "It looks like you split your lip."

"The dog..." he slurred. "I didn't see him."

Clive offered his hand. "Here, let me help you up."

John grasped his brother-in-law with one hand, holding the napkin to his mouth with the other. He stumbled. Clive steadied him.

"I think I hit it pretty hard," John said.

Donna approached. "Maybe we should go to the emergency room. You might need stitches."

"No! I'll be fine. It's just a little cut."

Clive helped him over to the couch. John fell onto the cushions.

Alex handed him a glass of water. "Here Uncle John, drink this."

"Can we at least eat the rest of the food?" Kevin called, still seated at the table. "I'm starving."

"Yes, of course," Helen encouraged. "Everybody eat! Dad's okay. We won't let a little spilled turkey ruin the meal."

Melissa nodded to Helen in approval. She turned to her sister. "Donna, we have an ice pack in the freezer. Can you please grab it?"

"Sure, right away."

"Eat," John mumbled. "I'll be fine. Just need to rest."

Melissa hesitated before she stood. "Okay. Call if you need anything. Alex, I know the kids would love if you joined them at the table."

"I will. Just making sure Uncle John's okay."

John shooed him away. "I'm fine, really."

Donna returned with the ice pack which John held to his lip. He flinched at the cold contact. "Sorry for ruining the dinner," he slurred. "Lately I seem to fuck everything up." A look passed between Donna and Clive. Pity? Whatever it was, they were in cahoots. It pissed him off. "You two in your big house and fancy cars don't have a clue what it's like to have your life taken away! Don't think I can't see the way you look at me, how you judge me."

Donna's eyes widened. "What are you talking about?"

"Take it easy, Buddy," Clive jumped in. "No one here is judging you."

Melissa appeared. "What's going on?"

John sighed with exhaustion. "I think I need to go to bed." He struggled to get out of the couch.

Here, let me help you." Melissa pulled him toward her.

He leaned on her as she helped him up the stairs. "I don't deserve you," he mumbled "You'd be better off if I killed myself."

Melissa gasped. "Stop it! I don't want to hear you say that again."

"It's true, Honey. You and the kids could have a better life without me."

"I mean it, John. Not another word."

Once in the bedroom, Melissa tried to help him undress, but he resisted. John didn't want her help. He could do it himself. Pulling the shirt over his head, he tried to avoid bumping his mouth, but it got tangled around his neck. He fought with it until he gave up and slumped on the bed. Melissa wriggled him out of it and took off the rest of his clothes. She covered him with a blanket. "We'll talk about this tomorrow."

"I love you, Mel," he muttered drowsily.

The kids were in the family room engrossed in *Jumanji*. The adults sat at the table eating pumpkin pie. They conversed in whispered tones. Everyone looked at her when she walked in.

"How is he?" Henry asked. Melissa noted the concern on his face.

"He'll be okay," she said. "He's been under a lot of stress at work. I think it may be catching up to him."

"Poor guy," Helen commiserated. "He's such a hard worker. Maybe he needs a little vacation."

"Maybe." Melissa sighed.

Helen rose from the table. "Henry, I think it's time we head home. Could you please get my coat while I say goodbye to the kids?"

"Sure thing." Henry stood. "Ladies, thank you for your hard work in the kitchen. And Donna, no one makes a better pie than you."

She stood and hugged him. "Why thank you."

Once her in-laws left, Melissa poured a cup of coffee and sat down. She hadn't touched her meal. Even the pie looked unappealing.

"Mel?" Donna said, "Clive and I would like to talk with you about something."

"Uh-oh." Melissa put down her cup. "Sounds serious."

They glanced at one another. Melissa sensed their urgency.

"Has John been drinking?" Clive asked.

Drinking? She hadn't expected this. "Of course not. He's been sober for years." Again, she witnessed a look pass between them.

Her face burned. "What exactly are you implying? That my husband is a liar?"

"No, not a liar." Donna's gentleness brought tears to her eyes. "We're just concerned about him, that's all."

Clive jumped in, "Why don't we make up the guest room and call it a night? It's been a long day for all of us."

Melissa agreed. She wanted nothing more than this evening to end.

Chapter 35

The telephone rang early the next morning. Everyone slept, but Melissa. She had woken before dawn after a restless night, unable to shake her sister's insinuation. Caller ID identified her mother-in-law. She snatched the receiver before it rang a second time. "Hello," she whispered.

"Oh, hi, Honey, I hope I didn't wake you. I just wanted to check on that son of mine." Melissa detected the worry in Helen's voice.

"Still sleeping," she said. "His lip was throbbing during the night, so we iced it again."

"I hope my call didn't wake him." Helen sighed. "You mentioned some stress at work, but Henry and I wondered if something else is bothering him."

Melissa swallowed the lump that rose in her throat. She wanted nothing more than to confide in Helen, to share this burden, but John specifically asked her not to mention it to his parents. In their mid-seventies, he wanted to keep their life worry-free. "I put them through hell," he had told her. "They don't deserve to relive this nightmare."

"Oh, he'll be okay," Melissa struggled to assure her. "I'll keep an eye on him. Hopefully, once this project at work is complete, he'll be able to relax."

The seconds ticked by before Helen spoke. "Melissa?" She paused. "Dad and I read about that darn registry in the paper. We're hoping against hope John's name isn't on it—not after all this time. But we don't have a computer. I didn't want to upset him by asking. Do you know anything?"

Her naivety so endearing, Melissa wavered between the truth and a lie. She exhaled. "He didn't want to upset you, but yes, his name is listed."

"Oh Honey, I've been sick with worry. We're just kicking ourselves for not insisting he go to trial and get his name cleared. If we knew this would happen, we would've encouraged him to make a different decision, but at the time, well gosh, he was so young! With the possibility of jail, well, I wouldn't have survived if…" Her voice trailed off.

"It's not your fault, Helen. You did the best you could at the time."

"Oh Lord! I'm so sorry. How hard this must be for you both. Let's make sure the kids don't—"

Melissa cut her off. "We had to tell them. We couldn't chance them hearing it from someone else."

"Oh dear! My poor babies. How did they take it?"

"It's been hard on them. They love their dad. They don't want anyone to think bad of him."

"What if we hired a good attorney? One who could maybe get his name expunged? We'd be happy to help with the cost. For heavens' sake it's been twenty-two years! It should be easy to prove he's no danger."

Melissa perked up at the idea. She'd be willing to explore any avenue, pay any sum, even mortgage their house. "Thank you for offering, Helen. It means the world to me. Let me talk to John about it."

"Okay, dear. Let us know what you decide."

He's driving the car on Hwy 1. Melissa and the kids stare at the ocean. Suddenly the car picks up speed. They round a curve and the wheels on the passenger's side hang off the cliff. He struggles to right the car and get back on the road. His kids yell. Dad, slow down! The speedometer reads 80 miles per hour! He slams his foot on the brake, flattening it to the floor. A sharp turn comes into view. Melissa, white as a sheet, screams at the top of her lungs. Oh God! We're all going to die!

John woke with a start. The sweat-tangled sheets wrapped around his body held him like a vise. Panicked, he tried to break free. His head throbbed. He wanted to stay in bed, but the clock flashed 9:20 a.m. He pulled on his Adidas tracksuit and brushed his teeth, careful not to make his lip bleed. His mouth, red and swollen, looked like he'd been in a boxing match. John straightened his shoulders and walked downstairs. Donna, Clive, and Alex were loading their car. He stepped into the driveway and hugged them goodbye, hoping any words spoken the night before had been forgiven.

Melissa bombarded him with words the second the car cleared the driveway. She followed him through the front door and into the kitchen. It appeared she and his mother had come up with a plan. *Christ!* He turned his back to her and reached for the orange juice. "I don't want my parents involved." He took a long swig. The citrus burned and dribbled down the side of his mouth. "Shit!" He put his face into the sink and let the cold water run over his lip.

John didn't have much faith in the legal system, but his wife's eagerness clearly overshadowed his behavior from the night before. He'd been worried that his in-laws were on to him, but it didn't appear they expressed their suspicions to Mel. He grabbed the kitchen towel and blotted the side of his face. Although reluctant, he thought it best to jump on her bandwagon. "If we decide to do this, we do it on our own dime."

"Can we though? Call a lawyer? It's worth a try, don't you think?"

"I don't know if the attorney I used is still practicing, but if not, his office can give me a referral."

"So, you'll call and find out?" she pressed.

He hesitated, then nodded.

Chapter 36

I 'm sorry," the receptionist said. "Daniel Laughlin no longer works at this practice. He moved out of the area. We can offer a referral if you'd like."

"Thank you," John said. "I live in San Mateo now."

"Sure. What is your case regarding?"

God, he hated this. Even though this unknown person couldn't see his face, had no idea of his name even, he struggled to reveal the reason for his call. "I'd like to hire someone to remove my name from the Megan's Law registry."

John heard the clicking of a keyboard, imagining her disgust. "William Gallagher has a practice in Redwood City. "He specializes in sex crimes."

John blanched at the words. He wondered if he had the stomach to go through this again.

"Would you like his contact info?" she asked.

"Yes, please."

Melissa insisted on accompanying him to the consultation. John didn't want to argue. He appreciated her support but would've preferred to go alone. Not only did he want to keep this dirty part of his life to himself, but he also didn't want to see the disappointment on her face if nothing could be done. Pulling their car into the parking lot of Anderson, Bruner & Gallagher, she remarked on the building's prestige. *Yeah*, he thought cynically, *these attorneys make the big bucks*. Melissa took his hand. Together they walked through the front door.

The receptionist led them to Mr. Gallagher's office, where the attorney stood. "Nice to meet you. He reached to shake their hands. You can call me Bill."

The smell of Old English furniture polish lingered in the air. John studied the deep brown mahogany furniture. Gallagher's huge desk and credenza, accented by the room's heavy dark curtains gave the impression of old money. A dark red Persian rug covered the hardwood floor, adding the only color to the room.

"What can I help you with today?" Bill gestured to the chairs in front of his desk. A shock of white hair, ruddy cheeks, and blue twinkling eyes behind wirerimmed glasses made him think of Santa Claus, sans the beard. *Ironic for a sex crime attorney.*

"My name is listed on Megan's Law," John said, looking the attorney straight in the eye. He wanted to appear confident, not to be mistaken for a common criminal. "My conviction, a plea bargain, is from 1983. I haven't had a single incident in the last twenty-two years. I don't have to tell you what the publication of this database has done to my family. We're hoping you can help."

"What's the charge?"

"PC 288," he replied.

Melissa glanced at him. She had probably never heard this term before.

"I see." The attorney leaned back in his leather chair. "We've had success at removing some names from the list, but none under this specific category. The law is stringent regarding acts involving a child under the age of fourteen. I'd like to ask a few questions if you don't mind."

"Yes, of course," John said.

"It appears you're a family man. My guess is you're gainfully employed."

"Yes."

"Children?"

"Three."

"Do you have people who are willing to vouch for you? Write letters to the court expressing their confidence in you?"

John's stomach sank. Here it was again. The thought of airing his dirty laundry, and asking others for help, made him want to get up and leave.

"We do," Melissa said. "My sister has known John since we met. Her husband, too. Is it okay to ask family members?"

"Relatives are good," Bill said, "especially if they entrust their children with you. The judge tends to take a closer look if the letter mentions one's line of work, education, accomplishments—that sort of thing. It helps to have a pool of competent people supporting you."

"My friend, Paul." John found his voice. "He's a reputable guy. I've known him for years. He works as a counselor in a treatment center."

"Another good one," the attorney said. "How old are the kids?"

"Fifteen, thirteen, and five," John said.

"How would you feel about asking the two older children to write a letter, attesting to the kind of father you are? I presume they know?"

Melissa reached for his knee and squeezed it, sending him the signal she did not want them involved. "We prefer the kids stay out of it," John said.

Bill nodded. He'd been rigorously taking notes but put down his pen. "I'd like to be honest with you. I mentioned our firm has been successful in removing names from the registry, but none with a 288 conviction. Child molestation is a serious offense. The laws are tough. We may have a chance at removing your name from the website, but it wouldn't dismiss you from registering each year with the police department. I imagine the public knowledge is most difficult."

"It's all difficult," John said. "After twenty-plus years with a clean record, I don't want to register at all."

"I understand, and I'll do my best. You have a solid history of upstanding citizenship. You've lived and worked in the community for the last two decades—which is a plus. It's not a guarantee, however.

Guarantee. Sweat broke out on his forehead at the mention of this word, conjuring memories of why he took the plea bargain in the first place. His option for the safe bet seemed ludicrous now.

"I assume you attended a court-mandated rehabilitation program?" Mr. Gallagher asked.

"Yes," John said. "I attended Bridges to Recovery every week for three years. I never missed a meeting."

Melissa looked at him quizzically. She wouldn't know about this. He finished the program before meeting her. "Before that I completed a 28-day drug and alcohol program at a treatment center. I've been sober ever since." He winced at the lie.

"Good," Bill said. "We can request your original court documents which should have this information."

Melissa leaned forward. "The people whose names were removed, what kinds of offenses did they commit?"

"Sexual battery by restraint, possession of child pornography, enticing a child into a house of prostitution. Rape."

Mel's mouth fell open. "Are you serious? Raping someone is considered less heinous?"

"Within certain circumstances, yes. The court draws the line at victims who fall under the age of eighteen."

"But someone who rapes a person over the age of eighteen has a better shot at getting removed?"

"In some cases, yes."

"Unbelievable," she sneered.

John squirmed. Hearing words like "child pornography" and "rape" reminded his wife that he fell into categories such as these. It shamed him.

"As I mentioned," Mr. Gallagher continued, "the court doesn't look favorably on crimes involving children. I want to be clear about this so you can make an informed decision. I can't promise you anything, except to assure you that I will present the best possible case. Hopefully, it will prove you are not a threat to society, and therefore not a candidate for the online registry. If you would like me to represent you, I require a twenty-five-hundred-dollar retainer fee. I bill hourly at a rate of three hundred dollars."

Melissa inhaled sharply. John knew it was more money than she expected.

"Your case is straightforward, so I don't anticipate my time exceeding the retainer. The judge will either agree to our argument, or not. You do the necessary footwork of gathering letters to support your character, and I'll contact the law firm that initially handled your case. Once I receive all documentation, I'll submit a packet to the judge for review before the hearing."

"Who'll be there?" Melissa asked. "At the hearing, I mean?"

"I will request a closed courtroom," the attorney said.

John looked at Melissa, his eyes inquiring.

"Yes," she said. "We'll do it."

"Very well. If you are prepared to pay the retainer, I'll have my secretary bring the paperwork in for your signature."

In response, John reached into his back pocket and pulled out their checkbook. Twenty-five hundred dollars would be a chunk out of their savings.

"Please make the check payable to Law Offices of Anderson, Bruner & Gallagher."

Chapter 37

Melissa hadn't spoken to Donna in two weeks. She'd called twice, but Melissa let the calls go to voicemail. Her accusation of John on Thanksgiving didn't sit right. Yes, he'd been off, but Melissa attributed it to the amount of stress they were under. Still, the comment nagged at her. She now watched him like a hawk, searching for telltale signs—slurred words or alcohol on his breath, but hadn't witnessed anything unusual. She dialed her sister's number. "Hi, it's me."

"Hi!" Donna greeted her. "How are you?"

Relieved to hear her sister's welcoming tone, Melissa released a heavy sigh. "I'm okay." Met with silence, she continued, "We hired a lawyer who may be able to get John's name removed from the website. I don't want to get my hopes up, but my fingers are crossed."

"That's great news!" Donna exclaimed. "I hoped you'd call me back, but when I didn't hear from you, well, I wasn't sure if...oh well, it doesn't matter. What did the attorney say?"

"He suggested we ask friends and family to write references. I wanted to ask if you two would write a letter vouching for his character. You could mention how long you've known him, how he's been a good uncle to Alex, or whatever you think would show he's a decent man."

"We'd be happy to. When do you need them?"

"The sooner the better. The attorney will put together a case citing John's rehabilitation and advocate that his spotless record the past twenty-two years is proof he's no danger to society. We need the letters before we can submit the packet to the judge."

"Got it," Donna said. "I'll do it first thing. Other than this promising news, how have you been?"

"Good days and bad. I'm hoping a positive outcome will get our family back on track. The older kids are having a hard time. It's really taking a toll on them. They're at such sensitive ages. Between typical teenage angst, and watching their parents struggle, well, both have crawled into a shell. They're holed up in their rooms most of the time. All I get are grunts when they come out for meals."

"That must be hard," Donna commiserated. "My niece and nephew are wonderful humans. They're tough. Your family has a solid foundation. They'll get through this. Shitty things happen in life. It builds character. Look what we experienced with Mom. It didn't break us. It made us stronger."

Melissa sighed. "I wanted to spare my kids the pain we lived through."

"And you have for the most part. You've been a great mom, and the kids love their dad. Your love and support will win out in the long run. I'm sure of it."

"I hope you're right," Melissa said. Thanks for the pep talk. I've missed you. I'm so sorry about Thanksgiving. I've been walking on pins and needles since the article came out. I didn't mean to snap at you."

"No worries. I apologize for mentioning it. You know John better than we do. We jumped to conclusions and shouldn't have sprung it on you like that. Forgive me?" Donna asked.

"Of course. I know you were only trying to help."

"I'll get those letters to you as soon as I can."

Melissa hung up and sat for a moment. Spirits lifted, she decided to take a chance and call Vicky. The two met in a mommy and toddler group when they first moved to San Mateo. Vicky's children were the same ages as Kevin and Diana, and the two became fast friends. They didn't see each other as often as when the kids were young, but still got together for an occasional dinner or movie. Melissa had been afraid to reach out, worried she might know about John.

Vicky answered on the second ring. "Hello?"

Melissa heard trepidation in her friend's voice; her greeting more of a question. Of course, Vicky recognized her number. Melissa's words stuck in her throat before they tumbled out. "How are you? We haven't talked in forever and I just wanted to see how things were going."

"Maybe I should ask you the same thing."

Vicky's cryptic words confirmed Melissa's fear, but she pressed on. "Do you have time for lunch? Or coffee? We could catch up. Maybe later this week?" Papers rustled on the other end; Vicky sorting through mail or maybe folding the newspaper. Melissa's stomach sank. "If you're busy this week, maybe another time would be better?"

Vicky cleared her throat. "I'm not sure how to say this, so I'm going to come right out with it."

Melissa gripped the phone.

"Are you aware of your husband's, uh, past? That he's—"

"Vicky, if you just let me explain. Please." She cringed at the desperation in her voice.

"So, you do know." Vicky's tone was icy. "Have you known all along?"

Fury filled her. "John is my husband. We share everything."

"Don't you think this is something you should have told me? I left my kids at your house when we went out to dinner. Under his supervision!"

"Your children, my children, are perfectly safe with John." Melissa bordered on hysteria. "Do you think I'd marry a man I don't trust?"

"Honestly, Melissa, I don't know what to think. How could you keep something like this from me?"

Tears sprang to her eyes. She tried to suppress the mounting sob.

Vicky continued. "Imagine how I felt when I scrolled through the site and saw his name. I was horrified! Now I'm questioning everything I thought I knew about him—and you. Phil has asked me to stay away from your family, and I tend to agree. We just can't be involved in something like this. I wish you well, truly I do." The phone clicked.

Melissa stood paralyzed; the receiver pressed to her ear. Soon she heard the steady hum of the dial tone.

Chapter 38

John left a message for Paul. He anticipated the conversation in his head, replaying answers to questions his sponsor might ask. He couldn't confess to blowing his sobriety, unable to bear the imagined disappointment in his friend's voice. And he certainly didn't want to listen to the obvious suggestion to plug back into AA. John wasn't an idiot. He knew what he should do, but he didn't want to. Drinking provided an outlet his family wasn't privy to. Everything else in his life had been put on full display—things once private, now public. He deserved to have something that belonged to him alone.

The phone's ring broke the commentary in his head. Recognizing Paul's number, John reached for the receiver. "Hey Buddy, thanks for getting back to me so soon."

"Always great to hear from you, my friend. How's everything?"

"It's been up and down," John said. "Challenging for sure. But I'm not calling to cry on your shoulder. I hired an attorney who may be able to get my name off the list. He suggested friends and family submit letters on my behalf, you know, tell them what a great guy I am." John forced a laugh. "You've known me the longest. I'm hoping you could write something about how I turned my life around, attest to the fact I'm a hardworking family man, that kind of stuff." He paused to take a breath, surprised by his nervousness. "Oh and write a statement about where you work and your job title. I guess a judge likes to know I keep good company."

"Would be glad to," Paul assured him. "When do you need it?"

"No rush, but sooner rather than later."

"Gotcha. How's everything else? You guys doing okay?"

"We're seeing a therapist," John snickered. "Mel's suggestion. I can't say I enjoy spilling our personal woes to a total stranger, but she thinks it'll help."

"What about you? Are you getting support?"

John had planned a response. "Yeah, I tried the meeting you suggested. It's good. It's close to home and gets me out of the house, out of my head." Never had he lied to Paul. His palms sweat from the deception.

"Good to hear. Hey, I'll mail the letter in the next few days. Sound good?"

"Thanks, Paul. I hate to get my hopes up, but if I could get my name removed, it would take a huge burden off the family. I want to do it for Melissa—for her and the kids."

"I understand." He chuckled. "I'll let them know what a terrific guy you are."

He hung up and buzzed Gail's office. "Hi John, what can I do for you?"

"Have you got a minute? I want to run something by you."

"Sure, come on over."

John stood and straightened his tie. He hoped his manager would agree to write a letter for him. Gail had a good standing in the community. She would be a great reference. Shoulders squared he proceeded down the hallway.

"We got the letters from my sister and Clive!" Melissa announced.

John had just walked in from work. He heard the excitement in her voice and pulled her from the stove into a bear hug. "Something smells good!"

"Kevin requested tacos with the works." She kissed him on the lips.

John's heart soared at this small act, her touch like a soothing balm. All the years they were married, how had he not recognized the extraordinary gift of a homecooked meal and a wife who loved him? Teary-eyed, he turned from her and grabbed the mail. "Oh, they each wrote one?" he asked in surprise.

"They did! Donna said she and Clive admire different traits in you. We figured the more letters, the better. She mentioned Alex writing one, too."

"Alex?" It was hard for him to imagine his nephew as a grownup, writing a letter on his behalf.

"Yep. Between their letters and Paul's...you talked to him, right?"

He nodded.

"Don't get mad, but I asked your parents. I know you don't want them involved with the lawyer stuff, but they want to help, explain their side of it, tell the judge how young you were, how they supported the plea bargain because it seemed the best decision, and how it turned out to be a dreadful mistake."

Although appreciative, John had a hard time accepting the generosity offered to him. What if everyone went to all this trouble and nothing changed? He couldn't bear the thought of disappointing his family again. He almost wished they hadn't hired someone. Living with the known reality of their lives, however difficult, seemed easier than having any newfound hope destroyed.

"Daddy!" Lucy called from her room. "Come see what I made!"

John smiled. "My other favorite girl beckons." He kissed Mel on the cheek.

Chapter 39

Melissa pulled out the Christmas decorations and loaded her holiday CDs into the disc changer. Johnny Mathis crooned, "have yourself a merry little Christmas" filling her with nostalgia. Her childhood holidays had been unpredictable due to her mom's depression. She and Donna made the most of it, but Melissa had longed for something she couldn't name. The first Christmas she spent with John's family thrilled her. She hadn't known how magical the season could be.

She opened the box marked *Ornaments*. Melissa savored the ritual of unwrapping each one, reminiscing how they became part of the family history. The first was a replica of the Golden Gate bridge stamped 1988. She and John purchased it in San Francisco on their first overnight trip. They'd stayed at a funky hotel on Lombard Street called the Marina Inn. Except for dinner at a Japanese restaurant two doors down, they never got out of bed. She chuckled at the memory, recalling the passion they shared before the kids came along.

Next came three "Baby's 1st Christmas" figurines, engraved with the year each was born. Her first baby would turn sixteen in a month. She couldn't believe Kev would be driving soon. Diana had matured remarkably this past year. Tall and stately, she showed no evidence of her once pudgy little girl features. And Lucy. How she loved this daughter of her heart. Diana and Kevin had each other, but Lucy was her constant companion.

She pulled out an ornament that displayed the American flag with a bald eagle perched beside it. "Colonel Brett Hillard, Marines 1982". A lump rose in her throat. He'd been a good dad considering his demanding schedule and living with a depressed partner. Diagnosed with cancer soon after she and John married, his chemo treatments overshadowed the joy of being newlyweds. John had been her rock during his slow deterioration. Melissa had cared for her dad, and John took care of her. She wiped her eyes and reached for the next box.

The aroma of cinnamon and vanilla greeted John when he arrived home from work. Scented candles illuminated every surface. Tiny white lights highlighted the nativity scene on the mantle above the fireplace. Ever since they'd met with the attorney, Mel had a lightness about her, a glimmer of hope. It scared him. He walked into the kitchen where she and Lucy wore matching reindeer aprons. His daughter, poised on a stool, stirred a bowlful of batter while Melissa held it steady. "My favorite girls." He kissed their cheeks.

"Daddy, Mommy's helping me make Christmas cookies for the class party tomorrow. I'm going to add all different colors of sprinkles to make them pretty."

"You're doing a great job, Lucy Goose. Your classmates will appreciate your hard work."

John stepped behind his wife. He pulled her close, feeling the length of her body melt into his. Pressing against her suggestively, he nuzzled her ear. "Last night was fun," he whispered, gruffly.

She turned to him, a slight blush on her cheeks. "Most definitely." Her smile highlighted mischief in her eyes.

He had gotten into bed the night before and was surprised when Melissa rolled over and straddled him. She pulled off her camisole, placed his hands on her breasts and groaned. Her fervor thrilled him when they kissed hungrily. He couldn't remember the last time she had wanted him. Their desire overflowed with an intensity reminiscent of the early days.

He stroked her cheek. "Can I help with dinner?"

"All under control," she said. "Kevin's playing video games, and Diana's at Marie's, so we'll eat when she gets home."

"Well, in that case, I'll take a shower and change into something comfortable."

"See you later, alligator," Lucy chimed.

He ruffled her hair. "In a while, crocodile."

If every day could be like this, he'd never want for anything. Mel's playful demeanor reminded him of their lives before the website. John wanted to ride this wave of hope as long as possible. Gail handed him an envelope when he left that day and wished him luck. Paul's letter had arrived yesterday. Once the character references were delivered to Mr. Gallagher, a court date would be scheduled. There would be no turning back. John wanted to savor this sweet time with his wife. If they lost, she might not recover from the disappointment.

Chapter 40

Mr. Gallagher reached out his hand. "Nice to see you again."

They settled into the captain's chairs in front of his desk, eager to hear the attorney's update.

"I've had a chance to read through the letters. You've got an outstanding group of people vouching for your character. I'm especially impressed with the letter your parents wrote. They succinctly laid out why they encouraged the plea bargain, despite your innocence, and their extreme regret considering what's happened."

Melissa glanced at him and squeezed his hand.

Bill flipped through the manilla folder labeled QUISENBERRY. "I have the paperwork from your case in '83. All the requirements of your probation were met, including the completion of the offender rehabilitation program. Other than this offense, which probably seems like eons ago, your record is clean. He set down the file. "You're the kind of person I want to succeed. I'll do everything in my power to put together a case attesting to the fact you're not a danger, but an asset to the community."

"Thank you," John said, unable to adequately express his gratitude.

"Do you have any questions for me?" Bill asked.

"How soon?" Melissa jumped in. "I mean, how long does it usually take to get this in front of a judge?"

"With Christmas around the corner, it won't be until late January."

She looked disappointed. John knew Mel wanted it done immediately. He, on the other hand, welcomed the relief of getting through the holidays on a hopeful note.

Mr. Gallagher continued, "My secretary will notify you of the date as soon as we get one on the calendar."

"Thank you again," John said. "We'll wait to hear from you."

Chapter 41

John's parents arrived bearing gifts. "Welcome to the chaos!" he greeted them. They stepped inside the entryway and barely dodged Homer. Reindeer antlers on his head, the dog chased Kevin through the house, rounding the corner so fast he slid on the tile. His antlers dragged across the floor. Kevin laughed hysterically.

"Melissa's in the kitchen checking on the roast," John said. "She put me to work peeling potatoes."

"Grandma! Grandpa!" Lucy shouted, running to greet them." Henry scooped her into a hug. "How's this big girl of ours?"

"I'm making cookies for Santa. Wanna come see?"

Henry kissed her forehead. "Absolutely!"

"Grandma," Diana called, "come look at this colored tinsel I got for the tree. I'm so sick of the same old silver every year. So boring."

"Be right there," Helen said, surveying the holiday decorations. "Boy, everything looks just lovely!"

"Hi Gramps," Kevin said, following them into the kitchen. "Mom, what time is dinner? I'm starving!"

"We'll eat by six." Melissa hugged Henry.

"Is there something I can eat now?" Kevin said.

Melissa pointed to the tray of appetizers. "Have a couple pieces of cheese and salami."

Kevin rolled his eyes. "I mean, like real food."

John ruffled Kevin's hair. "That is real food, my boy."

"Sure smells good," Henry said. "I've been waiting all day for this!"

Melissa nudged him playfully. "You sound like your grandson."

John sat at the head of the table. He watched his family as if an observer. Not able to shake the underlying dread of his upcoming court date, he wished he had a crystal ball to fast forward to next Christmas. Would they be together? He didn't know how Melissa would cope if they lost the case. She hung onto this shred of hope as if getting his name removed would solve everything. It wouldn't fix the damage already done. Those who believed him to be an offender wouldn't change their minds.

"Dad, are you listening?" Diana's voice snapped him back.

"Sorry, what was that?"

She sighed. "You were staring off into space. I asked if we could go to the bumper car place next week since school is out. I think Lucy is big enough to be in a car with one of us."

"Yes, yes, yes!" Lucy yelled. "I want to drive in the bumper cars! Can we, Daddy?"

"I think that's a fine idea." If only he could freeze this moment.

Chapter 42

2006

Cold January rain pelted the sidewalk. He and Melissa hurried to the courthouse. The gloomy forecast set the tone for John's anticipation of the verdict. His wife's optimism pained him. He could only imagine her devastation if they failed to win. She hadn't spoken a word since they arrived, as if realizing the gravity of this last-ditch effort. They were on the calendar for ten o'clock. Bill Gallagher planned to meet them fifteen minutes prior in front of the courtroom. Melissa sat stone-faced in the waiting area. John paced the corridor, dress shoes clicking on the Formica floor.

The attorney approached him. "You doin' okay?"

"Yeah, just nerves. Afraid of the outcome."

Bill sighed. "I hoped it would be a different judge, but Bruno's on the calendar. I won't lie, the guy is tough. I'm confident we have an exemplary case to put in front of him, but as we discussed during our first meeting, it's not a guarantee."

"I understand," John said. "Really, it's my wife I'm worried about. If it were just me, I could handle it, but if we lose, I'm not sure she can."

"Let's not worry about that yet," Bill consoled. He escorted John over to Melissa. "Good morning, Mrs. Quisenberry." He reached for her hand. "Big day, I know."

Melissa forced a smile. "Morning."

John heard the tremble in her voice.

"It's just about time," Bill said. "Are you both ready?"

Melissa stood. With shaky hands she smoothed the front of her outfit. She wore a gray skirt with black tights. A dark green sweater accentuated her olive eyes. Wearing the pearls he'd given her on their tenth anniversary, she looked stunning, yet not overstated. With solemn expressions, they entered the courtroom. John reached for her hand. His mind summoned images of the last time he stood before a judge. It staggered him that one stupid act would haunt him his whole life.

"All rise!" the bailiff announced. "This court is now in session."

They stood when Bruno Wilks entered. Gallagher had been right. His craggy face and bushy eyebrows gave him a hardened look. Grimacing when he sat, the judge's beady eyes searched the room as if looking over his flock. "Please be seated," he commanded.

John held tight to Melissa's hand to still his shaking.

The judge shuffled some papers and pulled out a pen. "I now call the case of John Quisenberry." His baritone voice echoed through the room.

Mr. Gallagher stood. He approached the bench, motioning for John to join him. Wilks peered over the top of his glasses. John swore he scowled at him. The judge then turned his gaze to Bill. "I've read the petition requesting your client be removed from the Megan's Law online registry."

"Yes, your Honor, that is correct."

"The case you've brought exemplifies your client as an upstanding citizen. The letters provided, which I reviewed, attest to his good character and family-man qualities. His employer claims he is hardworking and reliable, an asset to the company."

Sweat trickled from John's hairline down the side of his face.

He tried to follow where the judge was going.

Bruno set the file aside. "You are aware that any crime involving an underage child is the most serious offense?"

Bill nodded. "I do your Honor, however—"

"Save your speech, Counselor. While I appreciate the cost Mr. Quisenberry must suffer from having his name published, I'm not going to rule in your favor, and I'll tell you why. I don't wish to set a precedent of minimizing the magnitude of an offense against a child. I'm sorry, but your motion is denied."

Chapter 43

A dark gloom enveloped Melissa. The judge's decision was a kick to the gut, a crushing blow deflating all hope. And she blamed John. If only he'd been stronger, faced his accusers, fought for his future family. Of course, she knew that without the personal work he did in recovery, John wouldn't be the kind of man she fell for. She wouldn't have crossed paths with him or birthed her three beautiful children. Such a cruel twist of fate. Impossible for her to reconcile his past, she also couldn't bear the future repercussions.

They hadn't told the kids about the hearing, sparing them from possible disappointment. Melissa had imagined surprising them with the news that Dad's name would be expunged from the list. Together they would whoop, and high-five, relieved to return to the life they had known. Instead, the kids seemed to absorb her unspoken grief. She and John fought after every therapy session. One day they cancelled their appointment and didn't return. Couples went to counseling to resolve conflict, work toward a common goal. In their case, there was nothing to work toward, nothing to resolve. Unless she found peace with their lives on public display, she'd continue to live in turmoil. She didn't know how to hold her head high, to stand in the truth of her husband's character, while the world viewed him as a child molester. Daily she questioned her strength, belittling herself for falling short. Maybe John's remark during therapy was true. He had burst her bubble of a picture-perfect family. And she resented it.

Dark circles pooled beneath Melissa's eyes. Clothes hung from her once voluptuous body. She no longer tried to hide her pain from him. He should find another place to live. They'd be better off without him. John handed his glass to the bartender. "I'll have another."

Chapter 44

Melissa stood on a stepladder in the garage. She reached for the bin labeled *Sports*. Lucy asked her that morning to look for Diana's old skates. When she pulled it from the shelf, something came loose and rolled across the ledge. Setting the bin on the floor, she stepped back onto the ladder and ran her hand along the sides and back of the shelf. She grasped the wayward object and pulled it toward her. It took a moment to register the empty bottle in her hand. Heat rushed to her face. Something told her if she acknowledged it, named it for what it was, it would take her down a path from which she may not return. She removed the lid and sniffed. The residue of alcohol shot up her nose. Stunned, she methodically screwed the lid back on.

There had to be an explanation. She demanded her brain think of something. Maybe the bottle had been there since they moved in, left behind by the previous owners. Nonsense, she knew, but begged it to be something other than what she most feared. Thoughts of Thanksgiving hit her like darts in rapid succession. John's fall, his garbled words. Donna's insinuation that had made her blood boil. Her sister and Clive had been right. John had been lying all along. A slow-burning rage crept over her body. Bottle in hand, her legs shook as she climbed down the ladder.

Melissa walked out to the backyard and over to the turtle sand-box. John said they should just give it away since the kids had out-grown it, but here it sat. She lifted the lid and reached for the plastic dump truck, now brittle with age. Grabbing the pack and lighter from the cab, she sat on Lucy's play table and lit a cigarette.

"Honey, I'm home!" John called.

A gust of cold air from the front door chilled her body. Although trembling, she remained resolute. "In here." She barely recognized her voice, so tight and low, almost a growl. The empty Vodka bottle sat in front of her on the kitchen table.

John walked in and gave her a peculiar look. His eyes drifted from hers to the bottle. "What's that?" His face wore a puzzled expression.

"Why don't you tell me?"

"I'm not sure what you mean." He showed sincere confusion.

"What do you think I mean, John? Why is there an empty vodka bottle hidden in the garage?"

His eyes widened. "I have no idea!" He held out his arms and shrugged. "What, you think it belongs to me? God, Mel."

"Who else would hide vodka in the garage?" It was bad enough he tried to conceal it, but to look her in the face and lie? Who was this person standing in front of her?

"Did you ever think it could be Kevin's?"

His words shocked her like a slap in the face. "Kevin? Why would it be his?"

"Think about it, Mel. He's the same age I was when me, Kyle and Richard started sneaking alcohol. It's what teenage boys do."

Kevin? Her shoulders slumped, but a sense of relief washed over her. *The bottle might not be John's.* A second later she understood the alternative. Her eyes blurred with tears. "After everything you've been through," she cried, "why would he even try it? It doesn't make sense."

John took her hand. "I can talk to him when he gets home from driver's training. This is the kind of conversation a father should have with his son. I can tell him I found it—"

"No!" She slammed her hand on the table. "We need to show a united front. Both of us will address this together."

"If that's really what you want…" His voice drifted off. "I'm just saying that sometimes it's easier for a boy to confide in his dad when Mom's not around."

"No!" she snapped. "In this house, you and I are on the same team. The kids know they can't play one against the other." She observed John's hesitation before he nodded in agreement. He was preoccupied, distant. It troubled her.

"It's not mine," Kevin scowled.

"Son, you won't be punished if you tell us the truth," John said. "We just want to understand how the bottle got on the shelf in the garage. If you and Cole have been experimenting…" His voice drifted off.

"We haven't, Dad. Okay? I don't know how the bottle got there."

"Kevin," John spoke in a deliberate manner. "If it isn't yours, then whose is it?" He enunciated each word. Melissa witnessed a look pass between them, something she wasn't privy to. Warning bells sounded in her head.

"Mom and I just want you to be safe," John said. "You can take this as a warning if you tell us the truth. I know what it's like to experiment. It's hard to believe, but I was your age once upon a time." He chuckled and ruffled Kevin's hair.

Aghast, Melissa blinked hard. Was he honestly trying to be Kevin's buddy right now? Is this how they'd get the truth out of him? The exchange made her squirm.

Kevin put his head down. The room was silent except for the tapping of his foot. He appeared deep in thought. It took everything she had to wait for her son to speak. She wanted to tell him it was okay—that just this once they would forgive him. It would be so much easier if the bottle belonged to Kevin. If it wasn't his, she'd have to face the fact her husband was a liar. There would be so much more at stake. So much to lose. She shuddered. *What kind of a mother am I?*

"Okay," Kevin said, his voice resigned. "Cole found it in a cupboard at his house and brought it over. It was only one time. We didn't even like it. We were in the garage and heard the front door open, so I hid it. I planned to get it later but forgot. Can I go now?"

John looked at her as if waiting for a decision. Her stomach twisted, but she nodded, not able to meet either of their eyes.

Kevin slinked from the room. Moments later, his bedroom door slammed.

John rested a hand on her shoulder. She drew back as if touched by a red-hot poker. A look of surprise passed over his face. "Honey, he'll be okay. It sounds like it was just a one-time thing that he didn't even enjoy. He's learned a lesson. We won't need to talk about it again."

Melissa wanted to believe him, but a dark sense of foreboding brewed inside her, making her question everything. She gathered ingredients for one of Kevin's favorite dishes. *I'll show him he's forgiven.*

Chapter 45

His actions disgusted him. But, had he told the truth, the consequences would be dire. Surely Kevin understood this. He would talk to him when Mel wasn't around—admit his mistake and promise it would never happen again. Did Kev have insight into his sneaky behavior? Is that why he succumbed so easily? *I'll find a way to make it up to him.*

Behind Kevin's closed door, music blared. John hesitated a moment to gather his wits then knocked. "Hey, can I come in?"

The volume decreased a fraction. "Sure."

John entered the room and took in the scene. Kevin was playing Madden NFL on his Xbox while Green Day boomed from the CD player. The pungent odor of teenage boy invaded his nostrils. Heaps of clothes shoved into the corner emitted the smell of body spray mixed with sweat. A poster of Petra Nemcova, the Sports Illustrated swimsuit model, adorned his room front and center. He and Melissa exchanged glances when their son hung it up two years ago. "He's only thirteen!" she lamented. Now Petra stared at John with a smirk, as if calling him out.

"Son, I owe you an apology."

Kevin paused the screen but refused to look at him, the control gripped tight in his hands.

"There's no excuse for what I did. I pressured you to take the blame for my wrongdoing." John's face burned hot with the weight of his transgression. "I slipped up. I had a drink and didn't want Mom to know. She's been so edgy lately I couldn't bear to add one more thing to her plate. If she thought it belonged to you, well, I knew it would be easier. I could make her understand that boys your age experiment. She'd forgive you. Me, I'm not so sure."

Kevin looked him straight on, accusatory. "Did you leave it there on Thanksgiving?"

John grimaced. "Uhm, that obvious, huh?"

"You went out to the garage like ten times. When I asked what you were doing out there, you gave me a lame excuse. Then you dropped the turkey. You acted like you were drunk."

Confusion or anger, John wasn't sure which flashed in Kevin's dark eyes. "If Mom finds out, will she divorce you?"

"No, of course not," he said, "but she'd be very upset. I knew if you promised not to do it again, she'd get over it. I chose that over disrupting the whole family. I'm truly sorry I involved you."

Kevin stared eyes ablaze. "I won't cover for you again."

"You'll never have to. It was—"

"Dad. Stop. Seriously. I'm done talking about it."

John feared his son might hold this against him for the rest of his life. Honestly, he wouldn't blame him. "How 'bout we go to Best Buy later? We could get that new game you've been talking about. Residence of Evil? Is that what it's called?"

"Resident Evil," his son corrected with sarcasm. "Maybe. Can Cole come?"

"Sure! We can stop by Cold Stone on the way home. Get that triple-decker cone. How's that sound?"

Kev shook the hair from his eyes. "Okay, I guess.

Melissa knew it in her bones. Something was askew. Why hadn't John been more concerned? After everything he went through as a young man, suffering from alcoholism himself, why would he brush this off as simple teenage shenanigans? Was he trying to go easy on Kevin because of all the stress they'd been through? And Cole. It really stumped her that he would bring alcohol over. She trusted him. Loved him like another son. Cole knew they had an alcohol-free home. She would get to the bottom of this—find out what the hell was going on.

Chapter 46

"Hi, Mrs. Q!" Cole and Kevin burst through the front door. Sweat stained their *San Mateo Bearcats* jerseys.

"Hi, boys!" Melissa greeted them in mock cheerfulness. She'd waited almost a week for this moment. "Cookies just came out of the oven. They'll be cool in ten minutes!"

Cole grinned. "I smelled them when I walked in;"

Kevin stood in front of the refrigerator. "We're gonna play video games until they're ready."

"Correction," Melissa said. "The back lawn needs to be mowed. You promised to do it this weekend after practice."

Kevin opened a pack of DeliFresh ham and shoved several pieces into his mouth, then downed half a bottle of Dr. Pepper. "But Mom, Cole's here. I'll do it when he leaves."

"Cole can keep me company while we wait for the cookies to cool. The lawn will only take twenty minutes."

Kevin wiped the soda from his mouth with the back of his hand and dragged it across his pants. "Alright," he grumbled.

Once Melissa heard the door to the garage close, she turned to Cole. "Kevin told us about the alcohol." She planned to catch him off guard, observe his reaction.

Cole tilted his head. "Alcohol? What do you mean?" He appeared dumbfounded. Either that or he was a fantastic liar.

"Did you bring vodka into this house?"

He opened his eyes wide and stepped back. "No! I'd never mess with that stuff. Neither would Kevin."

Myriad emotions flooded her. She believed him. The truth that Kev hadn't been drinking made her want to weep with relief. Simultaneously, fury shook her as to what it implied. God, she needed a cigarette. Steadying herself against the counter, she turned to Cole. "Why would he say you were drinking if you weren't?"

"He said that?" Cole's face exhibited disbelief, but more than that, hurt.

"I think there's an explanation for his actions," Melissa said. "It's a long story, which I can't get into. Would you give me some time alone with Kevin? I don't want you to be angry with him."

He turned to leave. The bewilderment on his face crushed her. She rested a hand on his shoulder. "It will be fine," she reassured him. "We're going to work this out. Honest."

Cole walked from the kitchen shoulders slumped.

"Honey, wait." She wrapped some cookies in a paper towel and handed him the stack. "The chocolate should be nice and melty."

"Thanks," he mumbled.

Livid, Melissa sat at the kitchen table planning her next move. Lucy was on a play date till three. Diana and Marie were at the mall. John went to Yardbirds to get a new light fixture and would be home any minute. She needed the timing to be perfect.

The front door opened. "Do I smell cookies?" John called. He walked into the kitchen.

"Right out of the oven." She forced a smile.

He kissed her cheek. "Let me wash my hands. I'll eat one to make sure they're edible."

Kevin walked in the back door. "Done!" he announced. Clumps of grass stuck to his pants.

"You mowed the lawn!" John said. "Pushing that lawnmower will give you muscles like your dad."

Kevin scanned the kitchen. "Where's Cole?"

"He remembered he had to do something for his mom." She winced at the lie. "But since I have you both here, I want to run something by you."

"Sure," John said. "What's up?"

Kevin grabbed a stack of cookies and a carton of milk.

"Sit. Both of you." There was an edge to her voice. She saw John and Kevin look at each other, then back to her. They sat.

Melissa cleared her throat, "How is it that Cole knows nothing about the alcohol you blamed him for?" She sounded cool, in charge, though her heart raced.

Kevin looked confused. Then, as if registering a conversation took place in his absence, put his head down on the table. John's eyes darted around the room, the wheels in his mind appearing to turn.

"Well?" she demanded.

Silence.

"Honestly, neither of you is going to 'fess up to the truth?"

Kevin looked at her. Big tears rolled from his eyes, but he didn't speak.

She glared at her husband. "John, do you have something to tell me?"

Despair shrouded his face. "I can explain—"

"Kevin, go to your room!"

"But, Mom," he pleaded.

"Now!"

Her son stepped from the table, a look of fear in his eyes.

"Don't forget your cookies," she added, tenderly. Once his bedroom door slammed shut, Melissa faced her husband. "Do you want to tell me what's going on?" she spat. "Why our son got blamed for your bad behavior?"

"It was a mistake—"

Melissa cut him off. "What was the mistake, John? That you're drinking again? Or that you lied to me?" She shook with rage. "Or maybe it's that you coerced our son into covering for you?"

"All of it, I guess."

"You guess?" she shouted. "How long have you been drinking?"

His gaze fell to his lap. He wiped his palms on his jeans.

"How long?" she demanded.

"Ever since we lost the court case."

"Get out."

"John looked up in confusion. "What?"

"Get out!" She slammed her hand on the table.

"Mel, I—"

"No! I want you out. What you did is unforgivable. You blamed our son for your alcoholic binge! What does that say to him? The man I married would never, could never, do such a thing. I want you out. If you're having issues with alcohol, then you need to figure it out. I could have helped, supported you if I had known you were struggling. You didn't trust me enough to confide in me."

"Where do you want me to go?" he stammered.

"I don't really care. Get a hotel, call your parents—I just want you gone."

He stared in disbelief, as if seeing her for the first time.

"I'll pack a bag."

Melissa couldn't move from the table. Her entire body trembled. *How could I be so stupid? So blind?* She didn't know if her fury was directed at John or herself.

"Mom?" Kevin crept into the room. "Are you okay? Where did Dad go?"

"Sit down, Sweetie." She pulled out the chair next to her. "I'm a little shaken. Dad's going to take some time away."

"Where?"

She put her arm around Kevin and pulled him close. "I'm not sure. We need some time to think this through and figure out where we go from here."

"What does that mean? Think what through?"

"Honestly, I don't have the answers right now, Kevin. This is new territory for me, for all of us." She brushed the bangs from his eyes and tilted his head towards her. "What he asked you to do is not okay. I'm so sorry you were put in a position where you couldn't tell me the truth."

"I'm sorry I lied," he choked on a sob.

"Listen to me. You do not owe me an apology. You were put in a terrible predicament, and you did what you thought best. This has nothing to do with you." She kissed his forehead. "Dad would never do anything like this if he were in his right mind. The publication of that damn website has made him a little crazy. I didn't know he started drinking again. I blame myself for not recognizing he needed help."

"Will he get help?" Kevin asked. "If he promises not to drink again, can he come back home?"

Melissa didn't know how to answer his questions. The future of their family hung in a precarious balance, terrifying her. "Let's give it a few days and see what happens." She glanced at the clock. "I have to pick Di and Marie up from the mall, then swing by Camille's to get Lucy."

"What will we tell the girls?"

The maturity in Kevin's demeanor struck her. "I'll have time to talk to Diana after I drop Marie off," she sighed, "but I don't think I'll mention the bottle. I'll tell her dad's been struggling and needs some time away."

"She's going to ask why, Mom. Diana won't let you leave it at that."

"You're right." Her stomach sank. "I guess I have to tell her the truth." The thought of sharing John's failure with their daughter sickened her. "I just don't want her to worry."

"I'll talk to her if she has questions," Kevin said. "What will we tell Lucy?"

"I'll tell her he's on a business trip. Until we know more, I don't want to scare her."

"Sounds good. I can order a pizza for dinner if you want."

"Thank you, Sweetheart. I'll be back in a half hour." She pulled him into a hug.

Once in the car, Melissa collapsed into sobs.

Chapter 47

John didn't blame Mel for kicking him out. He'd assumed it was only a matter of time before the angst of the website got to her. It hadn't occurred to him his drinking would be the catalyst. He pushed through the heavy door to his hotel room at the Holiday Inn. The fake floral scent of cleaning products made him gag. He threw his suitcase on the bed and reached for the remote. Mindlessly, he flipped through TV channels. Not expected at work until Monday, the weekend loomed before him. Mel said she'd have supported him if only he had gone to her. The night he left after hearing of Kevin's fight, he'd told himself to get to an AA meeting. Instead, he ended up at a liquor store. Would he have told her if he knew? He didn't think so.

Melissa checked the flash of her cell phone: *Hubby*. Her breath quickened. She hadn't had an actual conversation with him in two weeks. The messages he'd left on her cell phone were rambling, incoherent. Shocked by his demeanor, she'd deleted them. They communicated by text only. When John came to the house to retrieve clothes, Melissa made sure she and the kids were out.

"When's Daddy coming home?" Lucy asked.

"I'm not sure, Sweetie. He's working on a project in San

Francisco." Melissa hated to lie, but her daughter was too young to understand. She helped Lucy call him at work a couple of times, which seemed to pacify her, though Melissa sensed her worry. The older kids did not express interest in speaking to him. Diana had clammed up since their conversation the day John left. Melissa had explained that her dad was taking time away to work on some things.

"What does he have to work on?" Diana asked.

"He's been struggling with alcohol," she'd said, a forced calmness in her voice.

Diana glared. "What does that mean?"

"The stress he's been under caused him to drink. He needs to plug back into AA and get support."

"Where did he go?" she asked.

"I'm sure he will let us know what he decides. He probably went to a hotel, or maybe to stay with Grandma and Grandpa."

"So, why does he have to work on it away from home?"

Melissa had put on a brave front. "Because it's not okay for him to use alcohol in our home."

Diana let out a snort and stared out the car window.

In the days that followed, Melissa tried engaging with her, but Diana shut her out. In contrast, Kevin became more talkative, even asking about her day when he got home from school. He took out the garbage without being asked. Checked all the doors at night to make sure they were locked. Because of John, their children had to worry about adult issues.

Melissa let his call go to voicemail.

John threw his phone across the room. "Dammit!" How long would Mel give him the silent treatment? He understood a few days, maybe a week, but ignoring him for two weeks irked him. He wondered how long she'd keep it up. His phone lit up with a text message: *if you want to get stuff, the house will be empty 2-4 tomorrow.*

Not even Homer was there to greet him. He walked upstairs and took four dry-cleaned shirts from his closet. Next, he threw socks and underwear into his backpack. If Melissa didn't let him come home, where was he supposed to do laundry? The bathroom smelled like cigarette smoke. Mel had the window open, but John didn't see anyone on the street below. He closed it and threw a pack of razors into his backpack. Who knew how long she'd ban him? He slung the shirts over one arm and headed down the hall. Passing Lucy's room, he couldn't help but go inside. Dolls and stuffed animals were strewn everywhere. Where did she think he'd gone? John knew his youngest daughter wouldn't understand his absence. It broke his heart.

He poked his head into Diana's room, and smiled at the neatly made bed, pillows arranged just so. So much like Melissa, his oldest daughter preferred everything tidy. John caught a whiff of strawberry shampoo and shuddered. Did Melissa tell Diana she'd caught him in a lie? He feared what she must think of him.

The door to Kevin's room was closed. Out of habit, John paused and knocked. Pushing it open, he came face to face with Petra in her swimsuit. Next month was Kevin's sixteenth birthday. John wanted to accompany him to the DMV, hand over the keys, and let him drive home. What if he missed this rite of passage? He sat down on Kevin's bed and wept.

Back at the hotel, John flushed the remaining alcohol down the toilet and looked up the address to the nearest meeting.

Chapter 48

Hi. My name is John. I'm an alcoholic."

Voices greeted him in unison. Hi, John!"

His body shook. Why had it taken so long to return? His resistance now seemed ludicrous. His marriage didn't stand a chance if he continued down the path he was on. John wanted to look Melissa in the eye and tell her with honesty that he had stopped drinking. As members shared their stories, John thought back to the friendships he'd made when he first got sober. Regret washed over him. Why did he let them slip away?

"Anybody ready to receive a surrender chip?" the secretary announced. "Who here has been sober twenty-four hours? Come on up."

Excited applause filled the room. A man with a long gray beard wearing a Harley Davidson jacket made his way to the front, followed by a woman, maybe in her twenties, sporting tattoos and piercings. Everybody cheered. John had forgotten about this ritual. He got his thirty-day chip while in rehab, but often witnessed newcomers receive a surrender chip at their first meeting. He counted back the hours from his last drink. Overwhelmed with emotion, he stood and walked to the front of the room.

After the meeting he was invited to join a group for coffee, but politely declined. He needed to get back to the hotel and make a long overdue phone call.

"Hey, Buddy," Paul's voice greeted him. "What's up?"

"What's up," John said, "is, well…I just got my first twenty-four chip." Greeted with silence, he knew his sponsor must be digesting the information. John didn't wait for a response. "I had a relapse. It took me until tonight to get my ass to a meeting."

"Why didn't you call?" Paul sounded surprised. "I didn't know you were at the end of your rope."

"Oh, I guess I couldn't bear to hear the disappointment in your voice."

"After what you've been through these last months," Paul said, "I would've been surprised if you weren't tempted to try to make it go away. I'm only sorry you didn't reach out."

"Honestly," John said, with sincerity, "I didn't want to be talked out of it. I wanted to just get blasted, my way of saying 'fuck you' to the world."

Paul chuckled. "And how did that work?"

"Just dandy," John said. "I'm calling from a hotel room because my wife kicked me out."

"Oh no! That's brutal. Is there anything I can do?"

"Nope, it's on me. I wanted you to know so I can be held accountable."

"Just remember," Paul said, "it's one day at a time, and you my friend, just got your first chip. Once you have some sobriety behind you, maybe think about becoming someone's sponsor. You have a lot of wisdom to offer others who are struggling."

"Yeah, maybe," John said. "First, I have to find out if Melissa will forgive me. I made a mess of things." His voice broke. "Not only did I let her down, but my kids have good reason to hate me."

"Let's focus on your sobriety. The rest will fall into place." Paul spoke with gentleness. "I'm here for you, Pal."

"Thank you. I appreciate it."

Despite the uncertainty of his future, John slept more peacefully than he had in months.

Chapter 49

As expected, John's call went to voicemail. He grabbed the hotel notepad off the desk and read the succinct script he'd rewritten several times: "Mel, I'd like the chance to talk to you in person, be honest with you, tell you everything I failed to express these last months. I'll understand if it's too late and will accept your decision, but I'd like the opportunity to apologize. Let me know if you'd be open to a conversation. I love you so much. Okay, bye."

Melissa listened to his message struck by the clarity in his voice—a sharp contrast to his previous ramblings of the last two weeks. She'd been mulling over her sister's suggestion that she and the kids stay with them in Pasadena while Melissa planned their next move. This of course would mean taking them out of school—moving them away from their father. She'd hoped it wouldn't come to that. The lucidity in John's voice inspired a glimmer of hope. She waited two days to see if her silence would be met with anger or emotional pleading, but John didn't call. Maybe he was ready to have a serious conversation.

She sent a text: *do you want to meet tomorrow while the kids are in school?* She got an immediate response: *Will take an early lunch and meet you at the park at 11. Thank you xo.*

Melissa's heart fluttered, surprising her.

Melissa spotted him at the picnic table where they'd sat several months earlier—the day they informed their children of the website. John stood when she approached. She could tell he wanted to embrace her but refrained. He motioned for her to sit. "I stopped at Golden Bell and brought your favorite donuts. In case you're hungry." He offered her a white bakery bag.

She took in his steady gaze. John's deep brown eyes fringed with dark lashes seemed to assess her, attempting to read her thoughts. His hair, graying at the temples, accentuated his handsome features. Melissa ached from how much she missed him—not the John of recent, but the man she fell in love with. She didn't reach for the bag.

"Mel, I've been a total jerk and want to apologize for my behavior. I'm one week sober—and yes, I'm counting. I had my first drink the night Kevin got into that fight. I lied to you about going to meetings. I went to bars instead. I hurt you. Deeply. I'm so very sorry."

Melissa refrained from speaking. She wanted him to divulge everything.

"What I did to Kevin, well...it's inexcusable. I lay awake at night hating myself. I was caught up in the addiction—lying and forcing my son to take the blame. I'd never have done such a thing otherwise. I know I can't go back and change the pain I've caused, but if you allow me the opportunity, I will do anything possible to earn back your trust. I'm willing to stay at the hotel for as long as you need, though I do hope in time you can find it in your heart to give me another chance. I want to come home."

Her face burned with emotion, livid at the deceit, at turning his back on her. And for what? Alcohol? She didn't know if she could forgive him. But what was the alternative? Divorce him? Start a new life as a single mom to three kids? That option terrified her more. She shook with rage. "How can I ever trust you again?"

John reached for her hand, but she tucked it into her lap. A look of sorrow passed over his face. "Mel, I can promise you I'm worthy of your trust until I'm blue in the face, but only time will prove I'm a man of my word."

"I don't want you back home," she snapped.

"I understand. We can take it as slow as you like. I'm not asking for a guarantee, Mel, just a chance."

Her heart pounded. It would be so much easier if she didn't love him. She could walk away, start a new life. And, painful to admit, it would be a relief to no longer be linked to his name. She regretted this truth, but honestly, his alcoholism was just the tip of the iceberg. Their family would still have to live with the consequences of his conviction; something she had yet to make peace with. But abandoning him to walk this path alone, tugged at her heart. If she decided to end their marriage, it couldn't be to escape the humiliation of carrying his last name.

"I need time to think," she said. "Before I make any decisions, I want to talk with the kids. You hurt them, John. I'll do whatever it takes to protect them from further pain. They don't deserve to be going through this, to have their lives blown up. They miss you, but I need to decide what's best for them."

"Of course," he said. "Whatever you need from me, I'll do."

In these words, Melissa recognized the John she loved. Despite herself, she peeked into the bakery bag. "Jelly or old fashioned?"

"Both." He grinned.

"So, you think you can bribe me with sweets?"

He kissed her hand. "It's a start."

Chapter 50

When's Daddy coming home?" Lucy stood before her, blankie wrapped around her wrist.

Melissa was running out of excuses. The house echoed in John's absence. The kids were sullen and cranky. She needed to talk to Diana and Kevin. It pained her to expose them to adult issues, but their childhoods ended when they discovered their dad was a registered sex offender. After she put Lucy to bed, Melissa called them into the kitchen. She put two steaming mugs of hot chocolate in front of them. "I met with Dad this afternoon."

Both kids turned to her, eyebrows raised.

"Is he coming home?" Diana asked.

"Not home, but I wanted to ask how you felt about seeing him."

"Is he still drinking?" Kevin asked, his tone surly.

"He said he hasn't had anything to drink in a week," Melissa said. "He's attending AA meetings every day."

"Does he want to come home?" Diana asked. "Or does he like staying at the hotel?"

"Oh, Honey." Melissa touched her daughter's arm. "Of course, he misses us and wants to come home. I just want to make sure he's ready."

"Is he?" Kevin asked. "Ready?"

"I can't answer that." She had to be honest. "Alcoholism is a disease, and a tough one to beat. I believe Dad wants to do everything he can to stay healthy, but his sobriety is up to him. Right now, it seems he's gotten it under control, but I'd like to give it more time before we make any decisions about him moving back."

"So, what does that mean?" Kevin asked. "He'd stay at the hotel and come for visits?"

"Maybe something like that," Melissa said. "We can start slowly and see how it goes. How would the two of you feel about that?"

"I guess it's okay," Kev said.

"Can he come for dinner tomorrow?" Diana asked.

"Why don't we call and ask him?"

John's cell phone buzzed. His heart jumped when he saw it was Mel. He cleared his throat before speaking. "Well, this is a nice surprise."

"I wanted to let you know I talked with the kids. We're wondering if you'd like to join us for dinner tomorrow."

He could barely contain himself. "Are they sure? I mean, are you sure?"

"The only thing I'm sure about is giving it a try. The kids want to see you, but they need you to be healthy. And we need you to stay sober. I'm willing to take it a day at a time and see how it goes."

"Thank you. I won't disappoint you. See you at five?"

"Sounds good."

She hung up before he could say, "I love you."

Lucy's little face peered out the window. A lump rose in his throat. She ran down the driveway and jumped into his arms. He held her close, silky hair brushing against his cheek. "Oh, I missed you, baby girl," he choked.

"Me too, Daddy."

When he set her down, she grabbed his hand. "Come see what Mommy and me made for dinner."

"Hang on Lucy Goose, let me grab something from the car." John reached for the bag containing a coconut cream pie and a gallon of ice cream. He handed Lucy a bouquet. "Honey, can you carry these to Mommy?"

"Oh, Daddy, they're so pretty. She loves the yellow flowers." Lucy skipped alongside him, eyes barely peering over the top. They walked through the front door. Melissa stood with the older kids as if waiting for a guest to arrive. "Here Mommy, these are for you," Lucy exclaimed. She handed her the flowers. "From Daddy."

John offered the bag to Diana. "I stopped at Heidi's Pies and bought your favorite. And ice cream," he added, looking at Kevin. He opened his arms to them. "Can I have a hug?"

They stepped towards him, wary.

"I'm so sorry." His voice broke. "I've let all of you down." He enveloped them in his arms.

"Dad, you're squishing the pie!" Diana scolded.

He wiped away tears. "Oh, sorry."

"Are you crying?" Kevin looked at him wide-eyed.

"I'm just happy to be home."

Chapter 51

Kevin pulled into the driveway honking wildly. Melissa ran through the front door. She'd been watching the clock since they left for the DMV. "You passed!" she screamed. John beamed. "With flying colors!"

Melissa jumped into the backseat. "How about taking your mom for a ride?"

"Me too!" Lucy yelled, running down the driveway. "I want to go, too."

Kevin grinned. "Get in!"

Once she and Lucy were buckled, Kevin turned to them like a chauffeur. "Where to, ladies?"

"Let's get ice cream!" Lucy shouted.

He put the car in reverse. "Yes, Ma'am!"

Melissa unrolled the window, delighted by the warm April breeze. Her heart soared, thrilled to be celebrating Kevin's accomplishment with John by her side. He had been there every evening for the last three weeks, joining them for dinner, helping with homework, and reading Lucy a bedtime story. Each night when she walked him to the door, it became more difficult to say goodnight. She wanted to feel him next to her in bed, share coffee in the morning, and discuss their day. The previous night Melissa cheered when John received a bronze one-month chip. If they were going to give it a try, it seemed right they live under the same roof.

John descended the stairs. Melissa sat in the living room sipping chamomile tea, while Simon & Garfunkel played on the stereo. John had laughed at her taste in music when they first met, but over the years he developed a fondness for her records. He sank next to her on the couch. "Lucy's all tucked in." He pulled her feet onto his lap and began to massage. Mel had always been a sucker for a good foot rub.

"Oh, I've missed this," she groaned.

John met her eyes. He whispered the words of the song to her, "I will ease your mind."

She smirked. "Well planned."

"Mel, I want to move back home and be a family." His voice shook.

"I want that too," she murmured.

John's heart lurched. He had been waiting weeks to hear these words. He pulled her down and stretched out beside her, melding his body into hers. Her breathing quickened with desire, fueling his passion. Ravenous, they found each other's lips, hands exploring every part of their bodies as if for the first time. "When will the kids get home?" he asked, breathless.

"Not till nine," she gasped, pulling off his shirt.

He reached his hands into the back of her leggings feeling the smoothness of her skin. Pressing her against him, a moan rose from deep in her throat. John stood, removed his pants, and knelt beside her. He rolled down her leggings an inch at a time, and kissed her belly, trailing his tongue to the spot that made her squirm. Tossing her pants to the floor, he brought her legs over his shoulders, pleasuring her with his mouth until she cried out. He pulled her down to the floor and knelt between her legs. Slowly, he entered her. It had been so long he wanted to burst but held on for as long as he could. Her hips rose to meet his, grabbing his buttocks, pulling him deep inside until his body wracked with orgasm. They lay panting in the comfortable familiarity of a couple who had spent nearly two decades together.

"Boy, I needed that," she giggled.

He grinned. "Happy to oblige."

Melissa propped herself onto an elbow. She brushed a lock of hair from his forehead. "I'd like to talk to the kids about you moving back home."

"I'd love that," he whispered.

"Daddy's coming home!" Lucy screamed.

A laptop hung from John's shoulder as he carried six weeks' worth of belongings into the house. His little girl ran to him. He knelt on the floor to greet her. She giggled and kissed his nose and cheeks. "I missed you, Alligator!" she said.

John buried his face in her soft curls. "I missed you too, Crocodile." He looked up to see the rest of his family standing in the wings. Brushing tears from his eyes, he set everything on the floor and embraced them.

Melissa kissed him and smiled. "Welcome home."

"I'll be down as soon as I unpack," he said. "Can't wait to shower in my own bathroom." He walked into the bedroom, letting the scent of his wife's Vanilla Musk wash over him.

Chapter 52

John hoped Melissa wasn't sorry that she took him back. He walked a fine line between gratitude and ambivalence, often wondering if he deserved to be home. The family's watchful eyes searched his every move, possibly looking for a crack in the veneer. He agreed when Melissa suggested they resume therapy. It would be a necessary step to heal their family.

"Good to see you again," Molly said. The therapist's gray-black hair was tied in a bun, loose tendrils escaping down her shoulders. She had a calming presence. John wanted to believe she could help them fix things.

Melissa brought her up to speed about his drinking, their separation, and his recent move back home.

"John, how has it been for you, being home?"

"I'm happy to be home. I missed my family." He paused. "But it's also strange."

"Strange, how?" Molly asked.

"I'm not sure I belong there anymore."

Melissa made a sound to jump in, but the therapist held up her hand to silence her.

"Tell me more," she said.

"Well, it sometimes feels like I'm walking on eggshells, like everyone is watching me, maybe wondering if I'm going to screw up again."

"By 'screw up' you mean drinking?" Molly asked.

"Drinking, lying—you name it. I was an ass."

"Do you fear you might start drinking again?"

"Not if I keep going to meetings and stay plugged in," John said. "I realize how important that is."

Molly turned to Melissa. "How do you think it's going since John's been home?"

"Well, I don't think anyone is waiting for him…" Melissa stopped and looked at him. "You," she emphasized. "No one is waiting for you to fail. I just think it will take time for the kids to trust you again—to believe you're here to stay."

Molly turned to him. "John, do you have insight as to why you started drinking?"

Of course, he knew. He had let his family down, disappointed everyone. His wife was desperately unhappy, and he couldn't make it better. "Well, sure," he said. "It was my fault that everything changed. I'd have done absolutely anything to protect my family, but it spun out of control. Like a freight train came out of the blue and knocked us to smithereens."

"How was it for you when you couldn't fix it?" Molly asked.

"I felt useless as a man. My job is to keep my family safe, and I couldn't do that."

"What about you?" she asked. "Where did you go for support?"

The room was still.

"I didn't want support. I just wanted to escape the pain. Once I started drinking, I hated myself even more. I'd feel guilty and try to make it up to them. When I couldn't, I'd get angry and drink again."

"It sounds like it was a hard cycle to get out of," Molly said. "I'd like to take some time during our next session to explore this further. Does that sound okay?"

They nodded.

Melissa wanted John to feel comfortable, but even after a month, he carried an aura of politeness, like a guest rather than a man who deserved to be at their table. Lucy hardly let him out of her sight, but a coolness emanated from Kevin and Diana. His attempts at conversation over dinner were met with one-syllable responses.

"Are you excited to be a teen counselor this summer, Diana?"

She didn't look up from her plate. "Yep."

"How many kids do you think you'll have in your group?"

"Usually ten."

"What about you, Kev? Are you going to help with the little kids' basketball team again?"

"Probably."

"I know how much they love when you coach them. With your experience, you may even get a paid job."

"Maybe."

Melissa saw the hurt in his eyes, but he turned to her and smiled. "Great dinner, Hon."

She often had to repeat herself when she asked him something—like his mind was elsewhere. Melissa understood it would take time to get back to normal, to build trust again. When she asked what she could do to support him, he'd sport a forced smile and assure her everything was fine. It became apparent there was a place inside of her husband she couldn't reach. Might never be able to reach again.

Chapter 53

Hey, we're going out after work to celebrate Eric landing the McMillan account. Want to join us?"

John stared at Beverly. Her bleached blonde hair was peppered with dark roots. The blue eye shadow creasing her eyelids gave her a clownish look. She hadn't initiated a conversation since the day he surprised her in Gail's office talking shit about his character. Yet here she stood at his office door. "I'm hoping we can move past that awkward day," she continued. "I apologize for the discomfort I caused. I admit I don't know the circumstances around your story. I've decided to base my opinion on what I do know about you."

John didn't know how to respond. *Thank you* or *fuck you* came to mind. He appreciated her apology, but the many times she had treated him like a pariah pissed him off. Being accepted by his colleagues was important to him. He recognized her invitation as an extension of the proverbial olive branch.

"Thanks," he said. "When and where?

BJ's Bistro drew a big crowd on Thursday nights, enticing the working class with half-priced beer and appetizers. John had accompanied his colleagues to lunch in the past but had never joined them for drinks after work. Melissa told him to have fun when he checked in with her. The night provided an opportunity to get back in the good graces of his coworkers.

The group was seated at a large table in the center of the room. They scooted their chairs to make room for him. John imagined a conversation must have taken place before they decided to include him. Maybe they sat around a table like this one, scrutinizing the details of his conviction. They could have deliberated like a jury, dissecting the facts, taking a vote. Although it appeared his coworkers came to a mutual agreement to overlook his transgression, he cringed at the thought of everyone discussing his personal business.

Eric grinned. "Hey everyone, beers on me!"

John remembered scoring his first account and understood his young coworker's excitement. He was happy for him.

"Everyone want one?"

"Sure," Beverly said. "Let's start with two pitchers and go from there." She reached her hand into the air and snapped her fingers at the waiter. "Two pitchers of Sierra Nevada," she instructed. "Put it on his tab." She pointed to Eric with a long red fingernail.

"Mugs for everybody?" the waiter asked.

A chorus of "Yes!" erupted.

He smiled. "Be right back with eight frosty glasses."

"May I have a glass of water, please?" John asked.

"Sure thing," the waiter said. "Would anyone else care for water?"

A few raised their hands.

John had almost said, "No mug for me," but as the only non-drinker in the group, he didn't want to draw attention to himself. It had taken time for his colleagues to tolerate his presence. He wanted to blend in, fly under the radar.

Eric stood. He was a short guy with a receding hairline despite his young age. "Allow me to do the honors," he proclaimed. Making a grand gesture of circling the table, he poured beer for everyone. John didn't say a word when Eric filled his mug. His colleagues raised their glasses in salute. All eyes were on him. Startled, John grabbed his mug and held it high. "Cheers," he joined in. *One sip won't hurt.*

As the evening wore on, more pitchers landed on the table. Exuberant amidst his buzz, John couldn't remember the last time he'd had this much fun. Laughing, and joking with people who appreciated his humor provided a sense of belonging. He stood to use the restroom and grabbed the table for support. How many beers did he drink? The thought threatened to suck the joy right out of him. He hurried to the bathroom and splashed cold water on his face. Staring in the mirror, he wondered if Melissa would be able to tell he'd been drinking. "Fuck!" His heart pounded at the indiscretion.

Why couldn't Mel understand that it would be okay for him to have an occasional drink with friends? Maybe he could talk to her about it, not hide it this time. It was the secrecy that had made it appear illicit. If he openly had a beer occasionally, he didn't see how it would hurt. Back at the table, he signaled the waiter. "I'll have an order of garlic fries, please."

Whoops broke out around the table. "Someone is NOT getting lucky tonight," Beverly snorted.

John laughed out loud. He hoped the garlic would cover up his beer breath.

Chapter 54

John waved to his AA friends. "See you next Saturday."

He'd committed to daily meetings as penance, after the night out with his coworkers. Mel had been asleep when he arrived home. He'd slipped into bed, careful not to wake her. "I love you," she had murmured, then turned onto her side, molding her body into the curve of his stomach. He had breathed a sigh of relief. Next time, he might not be so lucky.

It confounded him he'd toyed with the idea of telling Melissa. Even worse, he had tried to convince himself that drinking occasionally would be okay. John had argued that he was a strong man, steadfast, and successful. He also knew alcoholism had nothing to do with will. For twenty-plus years he hadn't given much thought to his abstinence. Now the preoccupation with alcohol had become a daily battle.

Melissa asked him to stop at Safeway after his meeting. With a kid who ate as much as Kevin, they were always out of something. John approached the entrance and noticed a group of people soliciting signatures. Each wore a red shirt with the slogan "We Care!" printed on the front.

"Please sign the initiative for stricter sex offender laws," a man implored a woman with three kids in tow.

"Absolutely!" she said, gathering her children close. "Where do I sign?"

John stopped in his tracks.

"Sir," a middle-aged woman called to him. "We're asking for signatures from community members demanding sex offenders be prohibited from residing within 2,000 feet of schools and parks."

John's throat went dry. "Do you have a brochure I can review?"

She thrust a stack of pamphlets into his shaking hand. "Take some and spread the word. We want this on the November 2006 ballot. The state needs tougher laws for sex offenders."

He mumbled his thanks, trying to catch his breath. Once inside the store, the flicker of fluorescent lights disoriented him. Sweat dripped from his temples. John reached into his pants pocket for the shopping list but came up empty-handed. He patted down his shirt pockets to no avail. He stood frozen as shopping carts dodged past him. A voice bellowed, "Hey, buddy, could you get out of the way?"

John bolted from the store. He searched for his vehicle, unable to remember where he parked. Pulling the key fob from his pocket, he clicked the button and followed the sound to his car. Once inside, he locked the doors. The brochures, clenched in his hand, were damp and crumpled. Tossing all but one to the floor, he steeled himself and read:

Proposition 83, the Sexual Predator Punishment and Control Act, known as Jessica's Law, is drafted in response to the tragic story of Jessica Lunsford, a nine-year-old Florida girl who was kidnapped, assaulted, and buried alive by a convicted sex offender who had failed to report where he lived. If passed, the Proposition would create "Predator Free Zones" prohibiting any person required to register as a sex offender from living within 2,000 feet of any school or park.

The new law also called for prison instead of probation, and extended parole for certain offenses. It had been challenging enough to find a house located more than 1000 feet from a school or park. When Melissa fell in love with their house, John had calculated, and confirmed that Baywood school was 1,200 feet from their property. If this bill passed, his family might be forced to move. A chill ran through his body.

"Mom, when's Dad coming home?" Kevin bounced a basketball through the kitchen. "I want to meet James and Cole at the reservoir and need to borrow the car."

"He planned to go to the grocery store after his meeting, but maybe he had other errands. You can take mine," she offered. Kevin had been driving for three months without incident.

"Mom. Seriously? You expect me to pull up in a red minivan in front of my friends?"

"Suit yourself," she said. "Try calling him."

Kevin pulled his cell phone from his pocket and walked into the other room. She heard him leave a message asking John when he would be home, with a request to "hurry".

"I'm going to shoot hoops till Dad gets here, then meet the guys."

"What time will you be home?" The front door slammed.

A half hour later, John appeared in the kitchen, white as a sheet.

"What's wrong?" she asked.

Without saying a word, he handed her a brochure.

"What's this?"

"I'm sorry Mel, I'm so sorry."

Panicked, she skimmed through the words. "Oh God," she cried. "Are we within 2000 feet?"

"Yes."

"Why can't they leave us alone?" she cried. "What are we going to do?"

He put his arm around her. "I could move. You and the kids could stay in the house."

She stamped her foot. "I'm not going to break up my family because of this fucking law!"

"It might not even pass," John said. "It needs more than 300,000 signatures to get on the ballot."

"It'll pass." She sighed. "No doubt in my mind."

Chapter 55

I think he's drinking again." Melissa had waited until the kids were at school to call Donna. For the past week, John seemed distant, preoccupied. She knew that damn proposition had put him in a funk, but he also had that now familiar faraway look in his eyes when he spoke to her. "I don't know for sure," she said, "but he's acting like he did before I caught him."

"Have you asked him?" Donna said.

"It wouldn't do any good," Melisssa said. "He'd just deny it."

"Is he going to meetings?"

"He says he is, but honestly, how would I know?"

I'm just really pissed off at a legal system that continues to punish people," Donna said. "Can you imagine the stress John must be under with this pending proposition? I can't imagine how that man gets up every morning knowing that no matter how hard he tries, the deck is stacked against him. I know you're upset, and I don't blame you, but I also feel for John."

"It seemed like we had a chance before this happened," Melissa whimpered, "but if it passes, I honestly don't know if our marriage will survive."

"It's only July," Donna said. "You have four months to prepare for the outcome. I'd like to think there are enough decent people in the world who would vote against it."

"But in the meantime," Melissa said. "What if he's fallen off the wagon? That's a dealbreaker and has nothing to do with whether the proposition passes or not."

Donna sighed. "Give him the benefit of the doubt before jumping to conclusions. With that said, my offer still stands. Your family is welcome to stay here if you need a place to go. We have plenty of room."

The door slammed. Her son walked into the kitchen with a scowl. "I'll talk to you later, Sis, Kev just walked in."

Melissa took in her son's frown. "What's wrong?

"Where's Dad?"

"He took my van to get the oil changed. Why?"

"I found this." Kevin shoved a brown paper bag at her. "He's drinking again."

Unable to touch it, Melissa grabbed hold of the counter. She guided herself along the cool granite until she reached the table and slumped into a chair. It shouldn't be a surprise, but her body shook.

Her son's brows furrowed with concern. "Mom? You look like you're going to pass out."

"I'm stunned." Perspiration beaded on her forehead. "Where did you find it?"

"In his car. I left some CDs in there the other day and went to grab them."

She braced herself. "Okay, show me."

Kevin reached into the bag. He pulled out an empty vodka bottle, along with a stack of Prop 83 pamphlets. "I'm not sure what those are," he said, "but he probably meant to throw all of it in the garbage."

Melissa put her head in her hands. *Think*! Taking a deep breath, she looked her son in the eye. "Honey, please don't say anything about this, I—"

"But, Mom," he interrupted.

"Kevin, I need some time. Promise me you'll let me handle this."

"I just hope you know what you're doing," he grumbled. "I'm going to Cole's to spend the night. I'm not going to pretend everything is okay when Dad gets home."

"I understand. I'm sorry you're caught up in this."

Melissa waited for him to get home from work. The older kids were swimming, and Lucy had a play date with Camille. She paced from the living room to the kitchen, rehearsing her words, forming responses if he lied or begged her to forgive him.

The front door opened. "Hello, hello," John called.

The familiar sound of keys landing in the ceramic bowl Diana made him in third grade gave her pause. What she was about to say could change everything, undo her family.

"Hi, Hon, how was your day?"

"I have something to ask you," Melissa said, "and I need you to be honest with me."

He looked puzzled. "Okay."

"Are you drinking?" She had the empty bottle stuffed in the kitchen cabinet, ready to pull out at a moment's notice.

"Why would you ask?" he said.

"I just need you to tell me the truth. Are you drinking again?" She mentally prepared herself for a fight. His denials, her evidence.

He sat down at the table, defeat shadowing his face. "I am. I'm sorry."

His admission dumbfounded her. "What do you mean?"

"I'm an alcoholic, Mel, and yes, I'm drinking."

"But why?" It sounded like such a stupid question, but she needed to hear the answer.

"Come on, Melissa. Your question should be, 'Why not?' It's one thing to ruin my own life, but now I'm destroying yours. I can't stand myself—can barely look in the mirror. I'm tired, so tired of pretending everything is going to be all right. I can't do it anymore. I'm going to find somewhere else to live."

His level-headedness flabbergasted her. She couldn't find her voice. When had he come to this conclusion? The anger she held so close only moments before vanished. A deep empathy emerged. She scooted her chair close to him. "I don't know what to say. I expected a big fight, but now I just want to thank you for telling me the truth."

"I love you, Mel. I wouldn't trade our marriage for anything in the world, but we can't ever go back to the way it was. I think the kids have a better shot at living a normal life without this dark cloud hanging over them." He took her face in his hands and kissed her forehead. "You deserve to be happy."

"This is your home," Melissa said. "You shouldn't have to move." She bit her lip, nervous to broach the subject. "How would you feel if the kids and I went to Pasadena? Donna offered her place to us for the summer. It would give you time to get help."

He hung his head, picking at the lint on his trousers.

"Look at me," she whispered.

He raised his eyes and met hers.

"Our marriage doesn't stand a chance unless you're sober."

"When would I see them? The kids?" he asked.

"It's not that far. We could make it work. But John, you can't see them if you continue to drink."

His voice cracked. "I understand."

Melissa stood, crossed the kitchen, and opened the cabinet of baking supplies. She reached in the far back and pulled out a holiday cookie tin. From the corner of her eye, she observed him watching her. She popped the lid, took out her pack of Virginia Slims and a lighter.

He raised an eyebrow, eyes wide. "What are you doing?"

She lit the cigarette, leaned against the counter, and took a deep drag. Tilting her head back, she blew smoke to the ceiling. "No more secrets."

John looked at her in disbelief, then started to laugh. She stared at him in confusion, watching his stomach rise and fall. She burst into giggles herself. The two laughed until tears streamed down their faces.

Chapter 56

2007

Mel screams. *The house is on fire! Get the kids! John runs from room to room, searching. They whimper behind a locked door. He pounds and kicks and breaks the door into splinters only to find the room empty. Diana wails. Daddy, find us! John runs as if he's stuck in mud. Mel shrieks. Do something! We're going up in flames!*

The earsplitting ring from the phone jarred him awake. "Oh God, oh God!" he cried out. Once it stopped, his cell phone began to vibrate. He knocked over pizza boxes and empty beer cans looking for his phone. Grabbing it from under the coffee table, he looked bleary-eyed at the screen: *5 missed calls.* John threw his legs to the floor to steady himself. He pressed the number. "Mom?" his voice shook.

"Oh Honey, you need to come quick," Helen sobbed. "Dad had a heart attack. He's at the hospital. They aren't sure if—"

"I'll be right there," he stammered. "I'm coming."

"Please hurry," Helen cried.

John pressed his hands to his throbbing head and made his way up the stairs. Before turning on the shower, he popped three Excedrin. Teeth clenched, he stepped into the icy spray.

John could barely comprehend that the diminished man lying before him, hooked up to wires and tubes, was Henry. Seated at her husband's bedside, Helen stroked his arm. John took the chair opposite her. "What happened?"

"We had our breakfast, and everything seemed just fine. Dad went down to the basement to look for a magazine and I heard him tumble. I ran to the door…" Helen's voice cracked. "He was lying at the bottom of the steps. I called 9-1-1. I thought he had tripped, but when the paramedics arrived, they said he was in cardiac arrest. He was fine at breakfast." Her voice broke into a sob. "I just don't know what happened."

John hadn't seen much of his parents in the past year. The reality of their distance pained him. After Melissa and the kids left for Pasadena, he didn't stop drinking, and they didn't come back. By the time Jessica's Law passed in November 2006, his family had been gone four months. Ashamed to face his parents, he ignored their calls. "I'm sorry, Mom. I haven't been myself lately."

Helen gazed at him. His face grew hot with shame. He imagined how disheveled he looked. "Son, you need help." Her voice sounded firmer than how she appeared. Deep creases etched her face. "Please. I beg you."

John couldn't mistake the worry and disappointment in her eyes. She looked much older than he remembered. If Henry died, John would be all she had left in this world. He hung his head with remorse. "Okay." He hoped he meant it.

They took turns by Henry's side, his body hanging in the balance. John asked his mom to give them a few minutes alone. When she stepped from the room, he leaned in close. "Hi Dad," he whispered, "it's me, John. I know you're worried about Mom, but I promise to look after her." He imagined how shallow his words must sound. "I haven't been a good son, and I'm sorry. You've been a great dad and grandpa, and I never meant to hurt you. I hope you can forgive me." Hot tears streamed down his face. He placed his hand on his father's heart. "I know I've said this before, but I mean it this time. I'm ready to do whatever it takes to stay sober." His tears dripped onto Henry's hospital gown. "I don't want you to leave this earth without trusting me to take care of Mom. I can make you proud again." John registered the almost imperceptible squeeze from Henry's hand. He'd heard him. John placed his head on his father's chest and wept.

His mom hovered in the hall, appearing lost. He pulled her into a hug and breathed in the familiar scent of Oil of Olay. Helen trembled from head to toe. "I'm here, Mom," John murmured in her ear. "I'm not going anywhere. We're going to be okay."

She pulled away. "I need to go to him."

John went to the cafeteria and returned twenty minutes later. The medical staff surrounded Henry's bed. Helen reached for John's hand and pulled him close. "He looks so peaceful," she whispered. "I almost felt him wave goodbye."

Chapter 57

My friend! I'm thrilled to see your number pop up on the screen."

"I'm ready," John greeted Paul. "Honestly. I'm serious this time."

"Why now?" his sponsor asked. "I mean, tell me how you know this time is different."

"I've survived everything I feared most, and I'm still standing. Barely. My dad just died," he choked. "Melissa and the kids are living in Pasadena with her sister. I've lost connection with all of them. There's nothing left for me. But I still want to live."

His friend's silence plummeted John into the pain he'd tried so hard to avoid. His sobs filled the quiet space.

"I feel how hard this is," Paul said. "I'm so sorry about your dad. Your mom will need you now more than ever. And your kids will always need you. You're only forty-seven, my friend. You've got the rest of your life to look forward to. I have faith that you'll get back on track and show the world the man I've always known you to be. I've never doubted you, John."

"I'm sorry I've been out of touch," John said.

"If I can offer one piece of advice," Paul said, "I recommend you find a good therapist. It's great to stop drinking and go to meetings, which I trust you will do. Getting to the root of this pain will aid in your recovery."

"I'll consider it," John said.

"Great to see you again!" Molly said.

Her welcoming smile eased John's nerves. He glanced around the office as memories flooded back. Their marriage therapy had been tough. Mel was in so much pain, and he'd been an ass, tuning her out, itching to get to the bar. "I've been sober a month."

Molly nodded. "I'm happy to hear it. So, tell me what's been going on. It's been over a year since we last met. You and Melissa had just reconciled."

John sighed. "I had every intention of not drinking, but I blew it. I ruined everything."

"Go on," Molly said.

"Kevin found an empty bottle in my car. Mel confronted me and I admitted to it. We agreed she'd take the kids and stay at her sister's house for the summer. It seemed like a good idea at the time. I needed to focus on my sobriety."

"And did you?" she asked. "Focus on your sobriety?"

"I kept drinking."

And Melissa?

"She enrolled the kids in a school near her sister's house. That's when I knew she wasn't coming back. She asked for a divorce. I convinced her it was better to get a legal separation. That way she could remain on my health benefits and not worry about finding a job. So, as it stands, we're legally separated."

"What was going on when you started drinking again?" Molly asked.

"I went out with my coworkers and got caught up in the moment. I told myself one beer wouldn't hurt. Idiot." John hung his head. "Then Prop 83 happened. The increased laws prohibited us from living so close to a school. I lost all hope."

"All hope you'd stay sober?" Molly asked.

"All hope that Melissa would stay with me."

"You came to this conclusion, how?"

"It was obvious. Being forced to sell our home would have killed her."

"Killed her, or you?"

"All of us. Me, her, the kids. I mean, how can a family survive something like that?" John wiped the sweat from his forehead.

"You continued drinking because you believed your marriage was going to end, so, why not?"

"Well, not exactly." John picked at the lint off his trousers. "I knew if she caught me, she'd have a reason to leave. It seemed like the one thing I could control."

"And the sale of your home wasn't." Compassion softened her words.

"I wouldn't be able to bear it—to stand by while her heart broke." Hot tears dripped from his eyes. "It was easier to destroy my marriage on my terms."

Molly nodded but remained silent.

"And then my dad died," John sobbed. "I'd barely been in touch with my parents after Melissa left. I worked during the day, came home to an empty house, and drank until I passed out. I couldn't face anybody. I promised my dad on his deathbed that I would clean up my act and look after Mom. It's the only thing keeping me from picking up a bottle."

"And you've kept your word," Molly said. "I hope you recognize what you've accomplished."

John continued, "Melissa hired a U-Haul truck when she and the kids came for the funeral. She asked me to stay away while they loaded their belongings. 'It will be easier that way,' she told me. It was awful. Now the house is on the market."

"Lots of changes," Molly said. "I commend you for staying sober during this time of uncertainty. We can talk more about this at our next session. Does that sound okay?"

He nodded and stood. "See you next week.

John walked through the front door and stiffened. The house was a ghost of itself. He'd worked on clearing out one room at a time. Every drawer and closet contained bits and pieces of a life that no longer belonged to him. He'd piled everything into plastic bins and placed them in a storage unit.

He'd slept on the couch every night since Mel moved out. Her lingering scent in the bedroom reminded him of all he'd lost. He felt stronger after his session with Molly, able to tackle the only room left. His clothes took up one side of the closet. He gathered them in one big armload and set them on the bed. He reached for the box on the top shelf. Melissa saved all the cards and love notes the two exchanged over the years. It hurt his heart that she'd left them behind. He spread them on the bed and read each one.

At the bottom of the box lay a manilla folder. Curious, John reached for it. Sheets of notepaper in various handwriting filled the folder. He picked up the first page and read aloud: "My uncle is an amazing man who taught me to ride a bike and took me fishing. There isn't a mean bone in his body. He would never, ever hurt anyone…" John's eyes filled with tears. His nephew had written this to the judge. Why did he feel like he'd let Alex down?

He turned to the next letter. "My husband is actively involved with our children. They love him dearly. I trust him with their lives—my life. Nobody cares for us the way he does…"

Page by page John studied the words, *outstanding husband, amazing father, trustworthy man, model employee, great friend, loving son*. These sentiments, written by those friends and family members, solidified a truth that resonated deep inside. The people who loved him weren't ashamed of him. He'd carried that burden alone. Until he laid it down, he would never be free.

John met with Molly weekly. Together they worked to reframe the way John viewed his conviction. "The event you experienced as a young man," she said, "is only one piece of fabric woven into the entire tapestry of your life. You are not only a man with a past, but a man of substance who has experienced much success."

"It's hard to see any of the good stuff," John said, "when my name is on a sex offender registry."

"What about the good that came out of your arrest?" Molly said. "Your sobriety and personal accountability led you to a wonderful woman with whom you raised children. For the most part, you experienced a loving marriage."

John nodded. "I can see that. If I hadn't gotten sober, I never would have met Melissa or had the great kids I have."

"I'd like you to focus on the things you can control," Molly said, "like being a good father, even if you're not married to their mother."

"My kids won't talk to me."

"But that can change when they see that you've changed. Plus, you have a renewed relationship with your mom. Helping her navigate the next phase of her life is so important. You have many positive things to look forward to."

John sighed. He had a hard time believing things would get better.

Chapter 58

<hr>

Mom, I'm thinking of transferring to the office in southern California," John said. "I'd like to be closer to the kids." He'd been staying in his childhood home with Helen since the San Mateo house sold three months ago. Aside from the forty-minute commute to his office, he enjoyed being in a place without reminders of the life he'd lost.

Helen put down her fork and studied him. "You would consider leaving your job?"

"Gail told me about an opening in the Los Angeles area that I'm qualified for. She's aware of my situation with Melissa and thought I might want to consider the move. It's a manager's position. I think I'm up for the challenge." He reached for her hand. "What if we went together? Maybe find a house with a granny unit."

"Oh Honey, wouldn't that be marvelous? There isn't anything keeping me here. This house is too big for me without your father. And I'm so lonesome for my grandkids."

"Let me talk to Melissa," John said. "I'll see how she feels about it."

Helen gazed at the home she'd shared with her husband for more than forty years. John rested a hand on her shoulder. "Are you ready, Mom?"

"As ready as I'll ever be." She turned away from him and brushed tears off her cheeks. John understood. When he handed over the keys to the realtor, it felt like a knife to his gut. Once buckled in, Helen turned to him. "Onward and upward, my boy."

John popped Vivaldi's *Four Seasons* into the CD player, then squeezed her hand. "For Dad."

"Oh, Henry just loved this!" she exclaimed.

The violin concertos filled the car. Neither said a word until they pulled over for lunch at Andersen's in Santa Nella. It was a family tradition to stop for split pea soup and warm bread anytime they traveled south to visit Donna and Clive.

"Does the realtor know we'll be there this afternoon to pick up the keys?" Helen asked.

"She does," John said.

"And the moving trucks are scheduled to arrive tomorrow?"

He smiled. "They are." This was a big move for him. He could only imagine how difficult it must be for his mom. The two purchased a duplex in South Pasadena, an eclectic town twenty minutes from where Mel and the kids resided.

"I can hardly wait to see the kids," she said. "I've missed them so."

"I've missed them, too, though I'm not sure they'll want to see me."

"Of course, they'll want to see you!" Helen said. "It might take some time to warm up to you, but being close by will make all the difference. You'll see."

John's mind drifted to the last time he saw his family at Henry's funeral. Lucy held tight to Melissa's hand, while Kevin and Diana followed close behind. John rushed over at the sight of them. He must have looked disheveled because the older kids pulled back and Lucy's eyes went wide. He'd quit drinking just days before— fatigue and irritation a constant companion. Melissa offered an awkward hug. "I'm so sorry about your dad. We'll miss him."

"I'm so sorry about us!" he'd blurted, then babbled about making it up to her, saying he'd fix things. What an idiot. She had gathered the kids close and said, "Let's go find Grandma." She'd turned to him with a look of pity in her eyes. "Take care of yourself, John."

"Have I lost you?" Helen asked. "You seem to be caught in a daydream."

Startled, he shook his head. "Sorry, Mom. What were you saying?"

"I said, once you have the spare room set up, I'm sure they'll want to visit."

He was doubtful. "I hope you're right."

John held his breath. Would Mel even pick up the phone when she saw his number?

"Hi, John." She sounded calm—like he was any other person and not the man she once loved.

He let out the breath he'd been holding. "Hi, hello. I just wanted to let you know that Mom and I are all moved in. I set up the guest room for the kids to come whenever they wanted to—and Mom did the same on her side. We want them to feel comfortable. I want them to enjoy spending time with us."

"Have you called them?" Melissa asked. "They're never far from their cell phones."

"I have," John said, "but neither picked up."

"Try texting them. They aren't big on phone conversations." She snorted a laugh. "Don't take it personally."

John sighed.

"Lucy's here. I'm sure she'd love to talk to you."

He heard muffled voices. A moment later his youngest daughter greeted him. "Hi, Daddy!

Tears sprang to his eyes. "Hey, Pumpkin," he croaked. "You sound so grown up!"

"Mommy says I'm an inch taller since my birthday."

"I'd love to see you, Sweetie. Maybe you can come over for dinner now that Grandma and I are all moved in."

"Okay," she said. "Just ask Mommy when."

"I'll do that, Honey. I miss you so much."

He hung up and sent a text to Kevin and Diana: *Grandma and I would love to see you guys. Can you come to dinner this week? Save my number so you have it.* An hour later, Diana responded: *lots of homework, maybe next week.* Kevin typed one word: *same.*

John tried again the following week but was met with similar responses. He wasn't sure his children would ever forgive him. He'd been absent—indulged his alcoholism, didn't care enough to get his shit together. Why would they want to see him? "Stop it!" he chided. He had to be patient.

It took three weeks before his children agreed to dinner, and only in response to Helen's invitation. The older kids let out an excited yelp to see their grandma but seemed uncertain at John's presence. Lucy ran to him but noticed her older siblings hanging back. She hugged him with a reservation that broke his heart. He and Helen took them on a tour of both spaces. John had taken care to fill their rooms with items left behind at the house. He knew they'd outgrown most of it, but Diana's eyes filled with tears when she spotted the net hanging from the ceiling with her stuffed animals. Kevin walked over to a shelf filled with his sports trophies, touching each one. "My Nellie doll!" Lucy screamed. "I forgot all about her. Where'd you find her Daddy?" John blinked away tears.

Helen made the kids' favorite lasagna with garlic bread, but dinner was filled with awkward silences.

"Hey Kev, Mom tells me you got an after-school job at the auto parts store," John said.

"Yep."

"Nice to make some extra money. I'm proud of you."

His son tossed the bangs from his eyes. "Yeah."

John turned to Diana. "Have you made some friends at your new school?"

She didn't look up from her plate. "A couple."

"I've made friends, Daddy," Lucy chimed in. "I have a best friend named Kelsey. Her daddy doesn't live at her house either."

John cringed. "I'm happy for you, Honey."

Diana took her last bite and pushed away her plate. "I have an English test tomorrow, so we better get going."

Kevin jumped up. "Yeah, I have homework."

Lucy pouted. "But what about dessert?"

Helen stood. "Don't you worry, Sweetie. Grandma made a whole batch of snickerdoodles that you can take home with you. I know they're Mommy's favorite, so maybe you can share them."

In a flurry, the kids were out of the house before John had a chance to hug them. He shut the door and turned to his mom. His shoulders slumped.

"Well, it's a start," Helen said. She patted his arm. "They just need time."

Chapter 59

M om, what if we took down the fence in the back?" John asked. "Wouldn't it be more practical to have one big backyard than two small yards?"

"Oh, that's a wonderful idea!" Helen said. "I've got so many ideas to spruce up the back. I'd love a project. The weather's just gorgeous!"

With the fence down, Helen took the lead, choosing fountains, bird feeders, and flowers of every color. It tickled him to hear his mom sing while she tended the garden. Most mornings he meandered out to the patio upon waking to find her reading the *Daily Word*. She'd greet him with his favorite words, "I've got a fresh pot of coffee brewing." They watched the birds flock to the fountains, chirping, and splashing. "Smell this air!" Helen exclaimed one morning. "It's just heavenly."

"Mom, are you glad we're here? I mean, I know you miss Dad, but does this make you happy—being in this house in this new city?"

Helen set down her coffee and took his hand. "You know, I never imagined what life would be like without your father. I was accustomed to him making the decisions, taking care of everything, you know, that's what marriages from my generation are like. It never occurred to me it could be different."

"And?" John prodded.

"And…" Helen paused. "I miss your father every day, but what I have here, oh Honey, this is the life."

John's heart soared.

"What about you?" she asked. "Have you settled into your new job?"

"Well, you know it's more responsibility. I work longer hours, but my colleagues are great. Everyone has been very welcoming." What he didn't say was the relief he felt working with people who didn't know of his past. Or the sick feeling he carried that he might be discovered. "I appreciate the AA community here. It's so out-doorsy compared to San Mateo. I haven't played volleyball or kayaked since before I married Melissa."

Helen nodded approvingly. "Well, you look healthy."

John's skin had darkened to a golden tan. His toned physique was reminiscent of the body he had in his twenties. He even fre-quented juice bars—something he'd have scoffed at in the past.

Helen smiled. "I'm happy to see you out enjoying yourself." She tilted her head as if weighing her words. "Have you met anyone interesting?"

"As in a woman?" John asked.

"Well, it's been a while since you two separated. I just won-dered if anyone has sparked your fancy."

John noticed women giving him second glances, even flirting with him. It had been a long time since he felt desired, and although flattered, he didn't want to complicate his life. He savored the sim-plicity of living on his own. Plus, he didn't think he could bear to reveal his past to someone new. "I'm not ready yet, Mom. I'm en-joying the friendships I've made, but until I have the kids back in my life, I really can't think about anything else." Besides, he still loved Mel.

"I had lunch with Melissa and Donna today," Helen said.

John was at his mom's place for dinner. "How is she? I mean the kids?"

"Everyone seems to be doing well. Melissa said they're gearing up for school, and you know how excited Kevin is for football season."

John felt a pang in his gut. "I told him I'd enjoy going to tryouts." His voice faltered, "But I never heard back. It's the same thing with Diana. I sent her a text reminding her I hadn't seen her in weeks. Her response was, 'Maybe you should have thought of that before you blew up our family.' God, it pissed me off. But I had to admit, she's right."

"They just need time is all. Remember, they went to Pasadena last summer under the guise of a holiday. It turned into a relocation, and it's taken a toll."

And I'm to blame.

"Once they realize you're here to stay, they'll come around."

"At least they have you," John said. "I'm grateful for that."

She laid a hand on his arm. "And we're not going anywhere."

Epilogue

2012

John guided Helen from the parking lot through the boisterous crowd of college students and family members. "Whew!" she exclaimed, pulling a hankie from her purse. "I'm glad they're holding the ceremony inside. Honestly, I just can't take this heat! Are you sure you know where to go?"

"I'm sure if we follow everyone," John said, "we'll end up in the right place." They trailed behind the herd of people entering the Bren Events Center. Once inside, John gazed in awe at the sheer magnitude of the space. Pulsating energy filled the room. "Kevin said we have tickets waiting at the information table. Let's head over there."

"Well speak of the devil!" Helen exclaimed. "If it isn't our graduate!"

Kevin bent down and hugged his grandma. The gold sash draped across his gown read, "Irvine University Class of 2012". "Hey, Dad," he grinned. "I made it!"

John pulled him into a hug "I am so proud of you, Son." He noticed Kevin's girlfriend behind him and reached for her hand. "Leslie, it's so good to see you, again."

She squeezed his hand. "You, too." Her smile radiated her pride in Kevin.

Helen swooped in and grabbed her. "Hug me, Sweetie. We have lots to celebrate! This fine young man of ours is going to make his mark. You just watch."

Kevin blushed. "Grandma…"

"Oh, don't you be modest. A Business degree! Grandpa is looking down right now, proud as all get out."

John beamed. He enjoyed the relationship Helen had with his kids and their buddies. It wasn't unusual to arrive home from work and find a group of young people hanging out in the backyard. She celebrated their accomplishments and offered words of wisdom. He would be forever grateful she created the bridge that allowed his kids to find their way back to him. "Where do we pick up our tickets?" John asked.

"Follow me," Kevin said. He pulled Leslie close and guided them through the crowd. They stopped at a kiosk and Kev handed John two tickets. "Mom and the girls are two rows in front of you. Uncle Clive, Aunt Donna, and Alex are on the opposite side of the aisle. I couldn't get all the seats together."

Helen clung to his arm as John led her to the assigned row. His heart stopped when he spotted Melissa. Dressed in a lavender sundress, her auburn hair fell in waves below her shoulders. She looked more beautiful than the day they'd met. Mel caught his eye and waved. His daughters yelled, "Dad! Grandma! Hi!"

"Uncle John!" Alex shouted over the rumble of voices.

John turned to see the smiling faces of his nephew and in-laws.

"Great to see you!" Donna called. "Big day!"

"Pomp and Circumstance" blasted through the speakers. Goosebumps rose on John's arms when the graduates filed in. Helen squeezed his hand. "Oh, Henry would have just loved this."

The sound of clicking cameras reverberated across the lawn. Melissa and Donna took photo after photo, as John's underarms grew slick with sweat. Kevin put his arm around Melissa. "Leslie told her parents we'd stop by after the ceremony. They'd like to congratulate me in person. We'll be back in time for dinner."

"And we're heading home to change clothes and grab the pies," Donna added. "See you at five!"

"You're coming, right?" Melissa looked from John to Helen.

"We wouldn't miss it!" Helen exclaimed.

Diana grabbed her grandma's hand. "I want to take you for a ride in my new car. I'll pull around and pick you up."

Helen clasped her hands in excitement. "Oh, that sounds like an adventure!"

"I want to come!" Lucy said. "Maybe we can stop by the juice bar and get Gram some wheat grass."

Diana chortled. "I'm sure she'd prefer a berry smoothie."

John ruffled Lucy's hair before the girls turned to leave. Her coltish appearance lingered between little girl and teenager. It was hard to believe she was going into middle school. She'd been only six when they separated—too little to understand why her daddy left, but young enough to forgive him his past failures. Every time she threw herself into his arms, John sent up a prayer of thanks for his sobriety.

"Uh, hey, you guys," Melissa called after them. "Do you plan to drop me off? Or did you forget you drove me here?"

Diana turned around. "Oh right. It's kind of out of the way. Can you just come with us?"

Before Mel could respond, John jumped in. "I can take you home. I mean, I'm happy to drop you off."

"If you don't mind," Melissa said. "I've got things to organize before everyone arrives."

Diana pulled the keys from her purse. "Thanks, Dad. Wait here, Grandma. I'll only be a sec."

"She sure is proud of that car you bought her," Helen said.

"A Volvo is one of the safest," John said. "Mel and I wanted her to have something reliable to get to and from Northridge."

Helen smiled. "That's our girl. Ready to save the world!"

Diana majored in social work with an emphasis on drug and

alcohol addiction. Her choice of study didn't go unnoticed. She pulled up and tooted the horn. John helped Helen into the car.

"Have fun, ladies," Melissa said. She moved closer to him. "Where are you parked?"

"Not too far," John said. "I got here early to snag a shady spot." He pointed to his car and opened the passenger door for Mel. She glanced at him and raised an eyebrow. His face flushed. They spent time at Donna and Clive's for holidays and birthday celebrations, and sat together at their kids' events, but rarely were alone. John followed directions to the house she'd purchased after the sale in San Mateo. Pulling into the driveway, he felt the familiar lurch in his stomach. She had created a life without him. He turned to her. "So, I'll be back about five?"

"Sure. Sounds good." She stepped from the car. Before closing the door, she glanced up as if something had occurred to her. "John, you're welcome to stay. I mean if you don't have something to do before the kids get back."

"Oh," he startled. "Sure, that would be nice. I'm happy to help with whatever you need. He smiled. "Put me to work."

John turned off the ignition and followed her up the cobblestone walkway. She opened the front door, and they stepped inside. John stood in the entryway admiring the high ceilings. It was a modern open floorplan. A sharp intake of breath caught in his throat when his eyes landed on the vase Paul gifted them at their wedding. It resided on an oak coffee table unknown to him. Mel must have noticed his disquiet. "I always loved that vase, but if you would like it, please, take it. I know it means a lot coming from Paul."

"No, no. It looks perfect where it is. You have a beautiful home, Mel."

"Thank you. Can I get you some iced tea?"

"That sounds great."

They took their glasses to a screened porch and sat in overstuffed chairs facing the hills. John stretched his legs onto the ottoman. The scent of lavender wafted through the screen. He inhaled deeply. "What a day," he said. "One down, two to go."

Melissa smiled. "It goes by so fast."

The click of toenails broke the stillness. Homer rounded the corner, stopped, and stared, a puzzled expression on his face. "Hey, Boy. It's me," John soothed. Homer's muzzle had grayed, and skin drooped over his clouded eyes. He choked back tears.

"He's almost blind," Melissa said. "I'm not sure he can see you." She turned to the dog, "Do you remember Daddy, Big Boy?" she asked in a singsong voice.

John held out his hand. "Hey Homer, it's me," he coaxed. "You remember me, don't you Buddy?" Homer's stub of a tail wriggled. The dog approached, sniffed his hand, and licked it, his feet dancing on the floor. John wrapped his arms around his neck, tears flowing down his cheeks. "Oh, I've missed you, old man," he crooned. "I've missed you so much." Homer licked John's face over and over.

Melissa laughed. "Your mom tells me you got another promotion at work."

"I did." John wiped tears and dog slobber from his face. "It was a good career move for me to come here. But most importantly, I get to be close to the kids. The joy I see on Mom's face every time they come by to see her, well, I feel like I finally did something right."

"I'm happy for you, John. You scared me that first year after we moved."

"Yeah, I worried everybody. I'm sorry. For everything."

"No need to apologize," Mel said. "We all went through a rough time. I'm just relieved we're on the other side. I often wonder what our lives would look like if, well, if things had been different. I never believed something could happen that would change our family so irrevocably."

They sat in silence. John tried to imagine where they would be today if the registry hadn't been published. He guessed Mel was doing the same. John cleared his throat. "The website was the catalyst that forced me to come to terms with the shame I carried. It was like a cancer eating away at me. I wasn't aware of how serious it was." He stroked Homer's back. "Maybe I should have shared with you how much I struggled. Even going to the police station every year was a constant reminder that people viewed me as scum."

Melissa looked at him with compassion.

"You and the kids were excited to celebrate my birthday, and I appreciated it, truly. But I walked around with a pit in my stomach, knowing I'd have to stand in front of that camera. I had to force myself to be in good spirits so as not to disappoint you. Perhaps the burden wouldn't have been so heavy if I'd been brave enough to tell you. I denied the ugliness so you wouldn't think less of me. My therapist helped me admit to my long-held belief that I wasn't worthy of you."

"John," she started, but he held up his hand.

"Let me finish. As long as things were smooth, I could block out all the uncomfortable emotions I harbored. I hadn't known I was one crisis away from falling off the wagon. When everything blew up, I scrambled to make things right, but I didn't know how, nor did I possess the tools to stay healthy. And once you were gone, I convinced myself there was no reason to stay sober. I didn't care if I lived or died."

Melissa rested her hand on his knee. "I'm so sorry."

"Then I got the call that Dad was in the hospital. Mom needed me, and it felt so good to be needed again. I couldn't let her down."

"Helen told me you had a good therapist who she believes saved you."

John chuckled. "It was my wise wife who found her."

She raised her eyebrows. "Molly?"

He nodded. "It was easier to see a therapist who already knew my story than to start over with someone new." John took a deep breath, gathering his thoughts. "Working with her was tough. I didn't know if I would ever see the light of day. She referred to it as my 'dark night of the soul'. I ached for you and the kids, but knew I had to get right with myself before I deserved to have any kind of relationship with them. Until I let go of the shame and regret, I could never truly be free."

John took a long gulp of iced tea. His hands trembled.

"Learning to meditate helped. I'm still not sure if I'm doing it right," he chuckled, "but just being still and clearing my mind from all the negative self-talk gives me a sense of peace. It replaces the urge for alcohol. Molly helped me to see that addiction was not a character flaw, but just that, an addiction. She helped me to believe I was worthy of creating a good life for myself, even if it wasn't with you." His voice broke and he reached for her hand. "I am truly sorry for what I put you through. I hope you can one day find it in your heart to forgive me."

"Oh John, I forgive you." Tears filled her eyes. "The kids struggled so much when we moved. I thought I'd made the biggest mistake of my life. They were angry, I was confused, bitter even. It didn't seem like things would ever get better. One day I was on my knees, just filled with grief. I asked for a sign, anything to show me I'd made the right decision." She hesitated.

"And?"

"The phone rang," she said. "You asked if it was okay to move close to us. And then you and Helen were here, and it was such a relief. Even though we didn't see each other often, I didn't feel alone anymore. You hung in there when the kids didn't make it easy, proving to them, and to me, that you'd never give up. Our children began to trust you again. I felt their excitement when you made plans to see them. They looked for you at games and recitals, scanning the crowd for your face, and you showed up every single time, cheering them on. I watched their world become bright again. You are a wonderful father, John."

Their eyes met. She brought his hand to her heart. "I'm grateful you found your way back to us."

John could barely breathe. He reached for her. Mel allowed herself to be pulled into his embrace. Her heart beat fast. Or was it his? "God, I missed you," he murmured.

Homer nosed his way between them and licked their faces. He and Melissa giggled. John patted his head. "Yes Boy, we love you too."

Note:

On July 1, 2021, Senate Bill 384 went into effect, terminating life-long registration for ninety percent of California's sex offenders. Community outcry at the injustice of persons listed on the site for non-violent crimes demanded change. John Quisenberry's name was removed from the list.

About the Author

RJ Barclay was born and raised in Northern California. She has an MA in Depth Psychology and is drawn to writing about subjects often silenced by shame. She desires to highlight different points of view on controversial topics encouraging readers to explore their biases. *Guilt by Default* is her debut novel.

The author can be reached at **rj.barclay@yahoo.com**